THE BOOK OF HAATAN

Novels by John Michael Greer

Ariel Moravec Occult Mysteries

The Witch of Criswell

The Book of Haatan

The Weird of Hali

I – Innsmouth

II – Kingsport

III – Chorazin

IV – Dreamlands

V – Providence

VI – Red Hook

VII – Arkham

Others

The Fires of Shalsha

Star's Reach

Twilight's Last Gleaming

Retrotopia

The Shoggoth Concerto

The Nyogtha Variations

A Voyage to Hyperborea

The Seal of Yueh Lao

Journey Star

THE BOOK
OF HAATAN

An Ariel Moravec
Occult Mystery

John Michael Greer

First published in 2024 by
Sphinx Books
London

British Library Cataloguing in Publication Data

A C.I.P. for this book is available from the British Library

ISBN-13: 978-1-91257-391-2

Cover art by Phoebe Young
Typeset by Medlar Publishing Solutions Pvt Ltd, India

www.aeonbooks.co.uk/sphinx

CONTENTS

CHAPTER 1

A LESSON IN MAGIC

Wind laced with waterfront smells came briskly up from Coopers Bay past rows of old slate roofs and leaning chimneys as Ariel Moravec approached the shop. Tucked in between an urban hardware store and a downscale hair salon, it had a narrow front, just enough for one not especially wide plate glass window and a metal-framed glass door beside it. Two neon signs flickered in the window. One, vivid red, said OPEN. The other, white and purple, displayed an open eye surrounded by wavy rays, and below that, familiar words:

AUNT CLARICE

CLAIRVOYANT

SHE SEES ALL

The narrow street to either side led not quite straight between ranks of tall brick buildings through the heart of the old harbor district; little shops and cafés filled the street level spaces, stretched awnings overhead and sandwich boards on the sidewalk. Above, tall windows directed a supercilious gaze toward her from five and six stories up.

Though she'd only been living in Adocentyn for three months, Ariel knew the street well enough that it surfaced more than occasionally in her dreams. It still took her an effort to push through a moment of pointless panic, take the last few steps, and reach for the doorknob. The thirteen Septembers before that moment made the panic inevitable. She was about to begin another year of school.

It wasn't the kind of school she'd expected to attend when she'd first come to spend the summer with her grandfather in Adocentyn. The plan then was that she'd spend eight weeks in the strange old east coast city and then take the train back to her parents' house in suburban Summerfield, with community college or a low-wage job looming up in her near future. That plan hadn't survived much more than a week after her arrival. A cascade of events that still made her pinch herself in sheer disbelief—a witch's curse, a clairvoyant's uncanny knowledge, a hostile spirit she could hear and feel but not see—had shoved her out of the future she'd expected and into another, at once more terrifying and more enticing. She'd never looked back.

That meant she had a great deal to learn, though, and it was time to start learning it. She squared her shoulders and grasped the knob.

Plate glass in front of her mirrored her own image back: body thin and a little angular, light skin just slightly tanned through a busy summer, straight black hair falling to shoulder height, big brown eyes upstaging small nose and chin. Though her teacher had told her to wear casual clothes, she'd dressed a little more fussily than usual, choosing her nicest jeans and a powder blue blouse with a hint of lace at the neck to go with practical shoes and a shapeless shoulder bag. It occurred to her then that Aunt Clarice would notice the choice of clothing instantly, and see straight through it to the tangled hopes and fears behind.

Should have thought of that earlier, she reminded herself, and pushed the door open.

Inside, shelves loaded with candles and oils and trinkets filled most of the space between the long candle altar along one wall and the wood-framed glass case of more expensive curios along the other. Scents of herbs and hot wax elbowed their way past the old-building smells of brick and plaster and well-aged varnish. Ariel turned and closed the door behind her as quietly as she could manage, trying to keep the little cluster of bells on it from chiming, but the effort did no good at all. From the far end of the shop, Aunt Clarice's voice came through the near-silence: "Good morning, Ariel."

"Good morning," she answered, and wove her way through the shelves to the little alcove in back where Aunt Clarice did her readings.

For once, Aunt Clarice wasn't perched in her chair at the little round table in back. She was on her feet, getting a big empty glass jar out of one of the cases along the wall. A tiny, bird-boned old woman with dark brown skin and tightly curled silver hair, she wore a blue dress dotted with moons and stars and a gold and blue headcloth. She smiled at Ariel and then handed her the glass jar. "Here you go. And here—" She gave her a brown paper grocery bag with the top taped shut. Large and lumpy, it weighed next to nothing and had something in it that crackled slightly. "You know where the back room is, right?"

"Um, no," Ariel admitted.

A finger brown and crooked as an old twig pointed across the back of the shop to the far corner. "Right behind the statues. Through that and down the hallway. Cassie'll get you started. I'll be back in a little while." A gesture shooed her on her way.

The statues were on a shelf unit of beige enameled steel that sagged with age. It looked as though it might have belonged to a dime store back when there were dime stores. Christian saints, Hindu and Egyptian gods, and other figures Ariel didn't recognize at all pressed close against three-legged toads with Chinese coins in their mouths, sad-faced white cats who beckoned with one paw, and the three famous monkeys who saw no evil, heard no evil, and spoke no evil. Behind the shelf was a narrow gap which ended at an equally narrow door. Ariel fumbled with the bag and the jar, got a hand free to open the door, and then had to fumble again so she could reach the light switch and see her way.

The hallway was only about ten feet long. Wooden shelves propped up by metal brackets ran down one wall; the other had a door in it, open just far enough that Ariel could see bathroom fixtures inside. Past that was another door. As she approached it, trying to keep jar and bag balanced while still leaving a hand free, Ariel fretted about who Cassie might be. The only other person she knew about that worked at the shop was Tasha Merriman, who came in during busy hours to field phone calls and ring up sales while Aunt Clarice was doing readings for clients or other important work that couldn't be interrupted. Maybe, Ariel thought, Aunt Clarice turned her students over to someone else at first. Her imagination brought up images of a hard-faced disciplinarian waiting for her with a ruler in one hand. She braced herself, opened the door.

On the other side was a cramped little room with a light fixture hanging from the middle of the ceiling, two barred windows letting in gray light from the alley behind the shop, white plaster walls stained here and there with the marks of old water leaks, and a big wooden table covered with varnish so old it was nearly black. Half a dozen wooden chairs the same color nosed up to the table at random intervals. In one of them sat a girl around Ariel's age, short and stocky, with brown skin, wide cheekbones, long straight black hair tied back from her face, and big round glasses that made her eyes look several times larger than they were. She looked up, startled, from a paperback in her hands.

"Hi," she said after a moment of mutual uncertainty. "You're Ariel, right?"

"Yeah," said Ariel. She set the bag and the jar on the table, closed the door behind her. "You're Cassie?"

That fielded her a sudden luminous grin. "Cassiopeia Jackson. Yeah, like the constellation." With a laugh. "You can call me Cassie. Everyone but my mom does. Is that the St. John's wort?"

A moment of uncertainty passed before Ariel realized she meant the contents of the bag. "I don't know. Aunt Clarice just handed it to me and told me to come here."

Cassie nodded. "That's what it'll be, then." She got up, took the bag and opened it. Inside was a great tangled mass of some dried herb Ariel didn't recognize, whole plants with not much more done to them than shaking the dirt out of the roots. Vivid yellow flowers and a sharp scent like turpentine caught Ariel's attention.

"You know what to do, right?" Cassie asked.

"No," Ariel admitted, trying not to sound as flustered as she felt. "I've only been here for readings before. I thought I was coming here this morning to start studying with Aunt Clarice, and that's pretty close to all I know."

Cassie nodded as though that was the most ordinary thing in the world, waved her to a chair. "No problem. Sit down and I'll show you. We're supposed to garble this bag of St. John's wort. Have you ever garbled herbs?"

"No," said Ariel, sitting down. "Just plenty of sentences."

Cassie's laugh rang off the windowpanes. "Okay, good. Garbling's sorting herbs so you have the different parts in different piles and the broken and damaged bits aren't in with the rest of it. I'll show you."

Over the next ten minutes Ariel absorbed the basics of garbling herbs and, tentatively at first, got to work helping to sort the St. John's wort into piles on the table: intact leaves here, flowers next to them, stems a short distance away, roots over in another heap, broken and damaged parts in yet another. All the while Cassie kept a conversation going. "Great-aunt Clarice says you're new in town."

"Yeah," said Ariel. "I moved here just three months ago."

"Where from?"

"Summerfield." Bland suburban images freighted with old unhappiness surfaced in Ariel's mind. She shoved them aside.

"Wow. I was born here—okay, let's be honest, across the bay in South Adocentyn, that's where my dad's from and about half my family still lives there. If you haven't heard about Southies yet, you will." Ariel sent an uncertain glance her way, but Cassie's gaze was focused on the herbs on the table in front of her. "That's still kind of home, but we live in town now. My mom was born in Korea, though."

"I wondered," Ariel said, who'd noticed the little folds gracing her eyelids.

"You're polite. I had people at school sometimes walk right up to me and say, 'What the hell are you?' I just looked at them and said, 'Weird.'"

Ariel choked. "I did the same thing."

"Did you? Good. Why'd they go after you?"

A long list of reasons rose instantly in Ariel's memory. "I'm a geek," she said, pruning the list ruthlessly. "I like to say things like 'the cat's pajamas' and 'twenty-three skidoo,' and I read lots of old novels."

That got her a sudden sidelong glance. "What kind of old novels?"

"F. Scott Fitzgerald."

"We," said Cassie, "are going to get along. I love Fitzgerald. Have you been to the library here in town yet?"

"Just the Culpeper Hill branch."

"You ought to go to the main library downtown. Up on the fourth floor is where they keep the old literature. I call it the Unpopular Fiction section."

Ariel laughed, but said, "Fourth floor. Got it."

"You live in town?"

"Yeah. On Lyon Street, near the park."

"Sweet. I live with my folks three blocks downhill from there." She tilted her head. "Any chance you've seen somebody prowling around people's yards? With a mask over his face, like he's scared of the virus or something? My mom spotted him Thursday right by our house, and I heard somebody else talking about it yesterday."

Ariel shook her head. "No. That sounds creepy."

"Yeah, I know. One of those things." She shrugged, dismissing the comment. "So how'd you get a place up in the nice part of the neighborhood?"

"I moved in with my grandfather after I got out of high school."

"Your grandfather. Anybody I've heard of?"

"Dr. Bernard Moravec," said Ariel.

All at once Cassie turned on her. In a loud voice: "What the *hell* are you doing here?"

Ariel, taken aback, tried to think of something to say.

"I'd crawl over busted glass to get the chance to study with Dr. Moravec!" Cassie went on: "And you're sitting here garbling *herbs?*"

"He says Aunt Clarice is a better teacher than he is," Ariel said.

That stopped Cassie cold. "He said that?"

"Yeah. He says she's better at some kinds of magic, too. That's why he gets his tobies from her, and comes here to get a reading most Tuesday mornings."

Cassie opened her mouth, closed it again, then said, "Wow. I had no idea." She busied herself with the herbs for a moment, then went on: "I know great-aunt Clarice is kind of a big deal here in town, but to me she's always been Dad's little old aunt who has the rootworking shop up above the old waterfront."

Ariel nodded. "Oh, I know. Until I came out here Dr. Moravec was just the grandfather nobody in the family wanted to talk about much." With a little shrug: "I still don't know that much about what kind of magic he does. He's not the talkative type."

"I bet. He's got a reputation for that." A sidelong glance came her way. "Hasn't he taught you anything?"

Another shrug answered it, dismissing a galaxy of uncertainties. "He had me read a couple of books that just talked about magic a little, and a few days ago he handed me another book, something by Eliphas Lévi."

"Which book?" Cassie asked, stooping suddenly to pull a cell phone out of the purse beside her chair.

"*Dogme et Rituel de la Haute Magie.*"

Cassie gave her an uncertain look. "You know French."

"I took three years in high school. I didn't like it much, but my grandfather says neither of the English translations are any good, so—" She shrugged yet again. "Maybe all those French classes weren't as much of a waste as I thought."

"Dogmay," Cassie repeated, starting to type.

"In English it's *Doctrine and Ritual of High Magic.*"

"Gotcha." Cassie typed the name. "I know Korean and enough Italian to get by south of Coopers Bay, but that's it. I'll have to read one of the English versions." She put the cell phone away and started in on the St. John's wort again.

After a silence, Ariel ventured, "So you've known Aunt Clarice a long time."

"All my life. I remember her from holidays when I was little, and when I was seven and got strep throat she moved into the spare bedroom and took care of me for like two weeks. I still remember the taste of the medicine she made me drink." Cassie made a face. "It's horrible."

"Yes, it is," said Aunt Clarice.

Ariel, startled, looked up from the herbs in front of her. Cassie did the same thing, with a little squeaking sound in her throat. Neither of them had heard the door open.

"Down the road a bit I'll teach you both how to make it," the old woman went on. "There's nothing better for a sore throat." She glanced over the herbs on the table, nodded, and then turned to Cassie. "How did she do?"

"Better than I did," said Cassie, recovering her composure. "Just sat right down and got to work once I showed her what to do."

Ariel looked from one of them to the other. "So this was a test."

"You better believe it," said Aunt Clarice. "If you can't handle a little uncertainty you're not going to get far learning magic." She pulled out a chair, sat down facing them. "But it's more than a test. Quite a lot of what I can teach you is about herbs and what they do, and you can't learn much about herbs unless you get right up close and personal with them. Now that you've garbled a bunch of St. John's wort, we can start talking about what you can do with it. You're probably going to want to take notes."

Cassie stooped for her cell phone again. Ariel reached down into her shoulder bag, pulled out an old-fashioned stenographer's notebook with a pen stuck into the wire spiral. With three months of practice behind her, it took her only a moment to get the pen out and poised to write.

Aunt Clarice gave her an amused look. "Don't tell me you do shorthand."

The idea hadn't occurred to Ariel. "Do you think I should?"

The old woman chuckled. "Might not hurt." Then: "Oh, one thing before we get started. You two live pretty close to each other. I'm going to ask you to walk home together once we're done." A flicker of emotion crossed her face. "A neighbor of mine spotted a prowler with a mask over his face on March Street yesterday, right by Storey Avenue, and my reading this morning warned me that something's not right about that. Might not be anything you two have to worry about, but I'd hate to find out otherwise the hard way. Okay?"

A quick glance and a mutual nod settled the matter. "No problem," said Cassie.

"Thank you," said Aunt Clarice. She picked up a stem of St. John's wort, and said, "Now pay attention. You both have a lot to learn."

CHAPTER 2

A NAMELESS BOOK

T he last block of Lyon Avenue, before the oaks of Culpeper Park rose up in their autumn colors to bar the way forward, was lined by Victorian houses on both sides: a demure flurry of ornate gables, carved wooden bric-a-brac, and windows in odd places looking down at the sidewalk or off into assorted distances. After three months in Adocentyn Ariel knew all of them at a glance. The one that mattered most was the one she knew best, tall and neatly kept, with green clapboard siding, white trim, and three stone steps rising up to the front door. The black mailbox mounted on the wall beside the door carried gold letters: Dr. Bernard Moravec.

Inside the entry, familiarities waited: the big coat tree of oak and wrought iron, the stair rising to the left, a closet door to the right. Straight ahead an open doorway let into the parlor, offering a glimpse of mismatched furniture, overloaded bookshelves, strange diagrams in ornate frames. Her thoughts were still full of the uses of St. John's wort and the conversation with Cassie. As she closed the front door behind her, though, Dr. Moravec called out, "Ariel? Your timing's good. We have a case. How soon can you be ready?"

Her face lit up. "Ducky. Give me a minute to get my stuff."

The old man gestured at the stairs, and she turned and went up them at a trot. Once in her room, she shed the shoulder bag

11

she'd taken to Aunt Clarice's, got a different shoulder bag from the closet, and paused just long enough to pat the head of the big stuffed timber wolf at the foot of her bed. The wolf's name was Nicodemus, and it had kept watch over her sleep since the day she'd turned thirteen. The fact that Dr. Moravec had never mentioned its existence, though of course he knew about it, was one of the reasons Ariel adored him.

By the time she came back down the stair Dr. Moravec had come out of his study. Tall and gaunt, with hair and pointed beard and big bushy eyebrows the color of hammered silver, he wore jacket and slacks of black wool, a crisply pressed white shirt, and a bow tie the green-gray color of a winter ocean. He nodded to her, a typical greeting, and headed for the door. Ariel grinned and followed.

Outside, beneath a sky of broken clouds and a first scattering of fallen oak leaves from the park, an old black Buick Riviera waited at the curb. Ariel glanced at her grandfather, got a nod in response, and went around to the driver's seat while Dr. Moravec climbed in the passenger side. Doors closed, seatbelts clicked, and the engine cleared its throat and settled into a steady purr. Only then did Ariel say, "Where to?"

"424 Holly Avenue. East on Rose is the quickest way." With a fractional shrug: "It's walking distance, but privacy will be helpful."

Ariel grinned again and pulled away from the curb. "So what's the caper?"

"A stolen book," said Dr. Moravec, without a moment's surprise; he was used to Ariel's fondness for 1920s slang. "Handwritten in Latin in a central European black-letter script, inherited from a great-grandfather with a strange reputation. There's apparently some question about the title. The owner reported the theft to the police and the police called me."

"A book of magic?"

Another fractional shrug answered her. After a moment, he relented. "That's what we have to find out. Whether it's a book of magic; if it is, what kind of magic; and in either case, whether the person who stole it has any idea what it is and what to do with it. More often than not in these cases it turns out that the book's harmless, the kind of thing you can find in the stacks of the downtown library. But there are exceptions. Five years ago the city police called me in on a case like this one, and by the time we managed to get the book back two people were dead and another had to be institutionalized. It's anyone's guess if she'll ever recover."

Ariel gave him an uneasy look. "What was the book?"

"A sixteenth-century manual of witchcraft. Quite interesting, really. It contained a very detailed recipe for flying ointment."

She sent another look his way, baffled. "Like, actually flying?"

He chuckled. "Not in a literal sense, no. Flying ointments were full of hallucinogenic herbs. That's a good part of what witches were doing in the Middle Ages, you know. The stories about weird festivals on the Brocken and so on? Accounts of drug trips. The problem is that you have to watch the dose very carefully, or—" His gesture scattered lives to the winds. "But we can discuss that later. I'll need a little silence now."

Ariel nodded, kept driving. The intersection of Lyon and Rose loomed up ahead, marked by street signs and a familiar coffee shop. She slowed, made the left turn, headed east past a few more businesses. Beyond those was a neighborhood of three- and four-story houses of colonial vintage, clapboard-sided and slate-roofed, that started with single mailboxes beside the doors, then added more a block at a time. The old man beside her sat with closed eyes and hands folded in his lap, his face all but expressionless, his attention somewhere Ariel couldn't follow. Not yet, she told herself, and wondered if she would follow him there someday.

By the time Holly Avenue arrived the houses had started to shed their spare mailboxes as flats and apartments gave way to rundown single-family houses of a later vintage. As Ariel turned left again, her grandfather opened his eyes and said, "Park anywhere you can." That turned out to be easier than she expected: a car pulled away from the curb half a block ahead of them and nobody else got there first. Ariel parked smoothly, got out of the car, and followed her grandfather up the sidewalk.

Three months of practice as a novice investigator had taught her already to pay attention to small details, and she didn't neglect that habit as they approached the house at 424 Holly Avenue. The blue paint on the clapboard siding wasn't quite peeling but another winter would see to that; the curtains in the windows were cheap dollar-store stuff, sagging visibly from age and well faded by the sun; the narrow strip of front yard had been mowed recently, but the grass was thin and Ariel could see bald patches of bare dirt here and there. The stairs that led up to the narrow porch bowed down in the middle. The well-worn doormat had a Bible quote on it, As FOR ME AND MY HOUSE, WE WILL SERVE THE LORD, in place of the more usual WELCOME. Ariel filed the details in memory.

Her grandfather knocked on the door: three quick sharp raps. After a moment, a girl maybe ten years old opened the door. Blonde and thin, she wore a tee shirt with a half-illegible slogan on it and jeans with a hole at each knee. "Hi," she said. "Are you the detectives? Mom and the policeman are in the parlor."

"Thank you," said Dr. Moravec, unperturbed. "If you'll lead the way?"

The girl beamed, pulled the door wide to let them in, closed it behind them and led the way. A typical Adocentyn house, Ariel thought: stair and two doors off the entry, hardwood flooring, plaster walls, a scattering of modern fixtures trying in vain to hide the fact that the building was from an earlier century. A little picture of the Virgin Mary in an unfamiliar style—eastern European, she guessed—was less typical. The living room itself had well-worn furniture in it, a stained sofa, two mismatched armchairs, end tables with battered lamps, a bookshelf with religious books in it and a stack of library books in old-fashioned cloth bindings on top, an old china cabinet of dark wood with wood-framed glass doors above and drawers lower down, a scattering of children's toys in the room's corners. One of the two people in the room seemed to match the setting: a woman in her thirties, maybe, with muddy blonde hair tied back in a ponytail. She was dressed in worn jeans and a sweatshirt, and her broad face tensed with tangled emotions as she looked up from one of the armchairs.

The other person present was a tall muscular Hispanic man in a dark blue police uniform, sitting in the other armchair with a metal clipboard in one hand and a pen in the other. He got to his feet as the girl trotted into the room. "Dr. Moravec. Thank you for coming out so quickly."

"I'm glad to assist," the old man said. "You haven't met my assistant, have you? Ariel Moravec, Officer Tom Cabra."

Ariel shook the man's hand, put on what she hoped looked like a professional smile.

"This is Teresa Kozlowski," said Cabra, turning to the woman. "I was just taking down her statement. Ms. Kozlowski, Dr. Bernard Moravec, from the Heydonian Institution."

She stood up and shook Dr. Moravec's hand with visible reluctance, mumbling "Pleased to meet you" half under her breath. She shook Ariel's hand without a word, motioned toward the sofa to offer them a seat, made a shooing motion toward the ten year old, and then sat back down as though the effort had used up most of what strength she had. The girl nodded and left the parlor through an open doorway leading into the dining room further back. Ariel settled on a corner of the couch, extracted a spiral notebook and a pen from her shoulder bag, spotted the policeman getting his pen in position at the same moment, and suppressed a grin.

"Now," said Officer Cabra. "Ms. Kozlowski, maybe you can repeat what you told me."

"Sure." She drew in a breath, closed her eyes. "The book's been in the family for I don't know how long. My great-grandfather brought it from the old country, and it had—" Her face tensed. "A bad reputation. I wouldn't have kept the thing in my house, but my grandmother made me promise not to get rid of it. So I kept it locked in a drawer here in the parlor." Her gesture indicated the china cabinet. "I never mentioned it to anyone outside the family except the priest at church."

"If you don't mind," Dr. Moravec asked, "which church do you attend?"

"St. Adalbert's," she said, in a defensive tone that startled Ariel.

"Ah." Dr. Moravec allowed a fractional smile. "That will be helpful. I know Father Novak tolerably well; he's consulted with me in a few difficult situations. You might ask him about me sometime if you have the chance."

The effect of these words startled Ariel even more. Ms. Kozlowski's eyebrows went up hard, and then she relaxed visibly and whispered something under her breath that looked like a little prayer of thanks. "I'm very glad to hear that," she said aloud. "It's just—this isn't the kind of thing a Christian ought to have anything to do with, and I wish I'd had the courage to break my promise to Nana Urszula and get rid of the thing a long time ago."

"I quite understand," Dr. Moravec said. "Perhaps you can tell me a little about the book."

She looked uneasy. "There's—there's not much I can say. I never read anything past the title page. It's handwritten in ink in an old-fashioned style, and Nana said it's in Latin, which I don't know. The title's something like Liber Nathan— it's in really fancy old-fashioned lettering and hard to read. It's bound in brown leather, cracked on both edges of the spine, and it's about this big—" Her hands mimed a shape around five inches by eight inches. "I kept it locked in a drawer, like I said, and wrapped in an old canvas shopping bag."

Dr. Moravec nodded. "And what happened to it?"

"That's just what I don't know. I don't get into that drawer more than once a month or so—I keep financial papers there, that sort of thing. I unlocked it this morning to get out a new pad of checks and the book was gone. I asked Paul about it, and Lucy, and they didn't know anything. Of course Joey didn't know anything either, and so I called the police."

"Paul," said Dr. Moravec, "Lucy, and Joey. I don't think you mentioned them."

"Lucy's my daughter," Ms. Kozlowski said, managing a smile. "You met her at the door. Joey is my son; he's six." The smile faltered. "Paul Chomski is my brother. He's on disability because of his health, and he's been living with me for the last four years, since just after my husband died."

"I wonder if I could talk to him."

"I don't see why not." She turned in her chair and called out, "Lucy? Can you see if your uncle can come down to the parlor?"

The girl appeared again. "Sure." She trotted into the entry, and a moment later her footsteps sounded on the stairs.

"Perhaps you remember," Dr. Moravec asked then, "when was the last time that you unlocked that particular drawer."

Ms. Koslowski gave him a bleak look. "I think it was the twentieth of last month. I'm not sure, but I think that was the date." Her gaze fell. "I know that doesn't give you much to go on."

"Quite the contrary," said Dr. Moravec. "If it was stolen by someone who knows what it is and where it can be sold, it may have reached a book dealer by now, and one way or another they can be alerted. If it's in the hands of someone who intends to use it, that's a little more complex, but again the window of time's worth knowing."

She nodded. "Well, that's something. I'll pray to the Holy Mother that nobody does anything with it that they shouldn't."

"That strikes me as a very good idea," Dr. Moravec said.

Ms. Koslowski looked up at him again, startled, and smiled. "Thank you."

Footsteps sounded on the stair: Lucy's, quick and light, and then another set, slower, heavier, and halting. The girl came pattering into the parlor a moment later, and announced unnecessarily, "He's coming." She headed off into the dining room.

A minute or so later a man came in from the entry: a little younger than his sister, with the same broad face and muddy blond hair, but with a face that seemed tense and worn beyond his years. He wore worn slacks and a sweatshirt with a bathrobe over them, and walked with a cane, not quite steadily. Ariel, after a quick glance around the room, got up and motioned him to her spot on the couch. He sent a smile her way and sat down awkwardly, as though his legs weren't quite strong enough to manage the task.

"Paul," said his sister, "this is Dr. Moravec. He's a consultant the police call in for cases like this one. He'd like to ask some questions."

"Sure," said Paul. To Dr. Moravec: "I don't think I know anything that'll help you, but prove me wrong and I'll be delighted."

"We can hope," said the old man. "Perhaps you can tell me what you know about the book that's disappeared."

"Not a lot. I looked into it a couple of times when I was a boy—my grandmother Urszula Nowicki didn't keep it locked away, you understand, and she talked about it now and then, so of course I got stupid and sneaked a look when I could. Didn't do me much good. It was in Latin, I think, which I don't know how to read, and the only picture I saw was some kind of diagram with circles and squares and a triangle, nothing that made any kind of sense to me."

"Do you recall the title?"

That got a rueful smile. "You're going to think I was pretty silly. I never looked at the title page. I just popped it open in the middle and looked at a couple of pages."

Dr. Moravec nodded. "Can you describe it?"

"Sure. Brown leather cover, cracked on both sides of the spine, maybe eight inches high by five wide and about an inch thick. I remember the paper was old and stiff, and had brown spots all over it. Beyond that I couldn't tell you anything."

"And do you have any idea what might have happened to it?"

The smile vanished from his face. "I wish. Teresa's probably told you that my health isn't good. Fibromyalgia, a couple of autoimmune conditions—" He shrugged. "But you don't want to hear about that, I'm sure. The short version? When Teresa's working, Lucy's at school, and Joey's at day care, I'm usually asleep upstairs. If somebody knew what to look for they could pick a couple of locks, get in and get out with the book, and I'd have no clue."

"If they knew what to look for," said Dr. Moravec. "How would someone know that?"

Paul drew in a breath. "You'll probably think this sounds crazy, but I believe in the supernatural." With a smile toward his sister: "You kind of have to if you go to church, after all." Then, turning back to Dr. Moravec: "This isn't something I know much of anything about, but you hear stories. I think if somebody did some kind of rituals, they could find out about something like this. I think there are things that aren't human that could tell them. If you believe in God and His angels, it follows that there are—other things." Ms. Kozlowski closed her eyes and shuddered visibly. "Things you shouldn't mess with, but people get stupid." He shrugged again. "Like I said, you probably think that's crazy."

"Not at all," said Dr. Moravec. "Is there anything else that either of you can tell me?"

There wasn't. The old man glanced at Ariel, who finished writing down a word and then sent a nod his way. He got to his feet. "Thank you, both of you," he said. "You've told me more than enough to begin making inquiries. I'll let you know what I find."

The two of them answered with polite noises, Teresa Kozlowski distracted, her brother calm but obviously tired.

Dr. Moravec nodded to the detective and the police officer, and headed for the front door with Ariel at his heels.

He didn't speak until they were in the car and Ariel had started the engine. "Curious," he said then. "I'm not familiar with a *Liber Nathan*, or any other title that might be misread that way, but there are people who know more about the literature than I do." Once the Buick pulled away from the curb, he glanced at Ariel. "What did you notice?"

"They both know more than they let on," Ariel said at once.

"Good. Go on."

. She paused while turning onto Mallory Street. "Paul knows something about magic, I think. Not a lot, but something. Teresa knows something about what's in the book. They don't want to admit to each other what they know."

The old man nodded. "That's common enough in families that have a book of sorcery but don't practice. What else did you notice?"

"Not very much," Ariel admitted. "They don't have a lot of money. They're religious, but I think she's more serious about it than he is."

He paused, then said, "Did you notice anything about the lock on the drawer?"

"No. I don't know a lot about locks."

"We'll have to remedy that someday. That one was a lock in name only. A reasonably clever child could pick it with a paper clip, and any competent thief could have gotten it open in a fraction of a second. The front door has a deadbolt, but it's a cheap hardware store lock—again, no problem at all to a professional thief. Paul was right: if someone knew what to look for it would be an easy job to get it."

Ariel gave him an uneasy look. "Do you think he's right about how they found out?"

"Possibly," said Dr. Moravec. "But I'll want to rule out natural possibilities first, and that means paying a visit to Father Vincent Novak."

Ariel glanced at him, kept driving.

CHAPTER 3

A LOCAL LEGEND

"**W**ell, Mom's a mudang," said Cassie, as though that explained everything. Ariel gave her an uncertain look.

The two of them walked along Harbor Street into the teeth of a brisk salt-tinged wind, with the long slow cluttered rise of Culpeper Hill to their left and the rumpled blue surface of Coopers Bay on their right, stretching across to the cranes and container ships of the working waterfront on the bay's other side. Their second day's lessons with Aunt Clarice had been interrupted by an unexpected call from an influential client, someone from the neighborhood of big houses and old money near the Heydonian Institution, with a question sensitive enough that a reading had to be done in private. Since Tasha Merriman hadn't yet arrived for her shift, that meant that the shop was temporarily shut and Ariel and Cassie got turned loose for an hour.

"I know, we can go down to the waterfront and pick up a couple of bombs," Cassie said, and when Ariel sent a blank look her way: "You haven't had an Adocentyn bomb yet? Seriously? Wow. Come on, the best place on this side of the water is just a few blocks."

That sent them down to the waterfront, talking the whole way, mostly about Cassie's family. After Ariel deflected a couple of questions about hers, Cassie glanced at her, nodded, and let that subject drop.

"Okay," said Ariel. "What's a mudang?"

"A shaman, kind of. Mom's family has been mudangs since I don't know when—some mudangs are like that, hereditary. Her mom, my grandma Chung-hwae, is a really famous mudang, and that's how Mom and Dad met." She turned suddenly toward the water, and Ariel nearly ran into her. "Here we go. Not too much of a line, either."

Ten people stood in front of them in an uneven line stretching from the sidewalk across part of an old wharf to a little shack with nothing behind it but a long drop into salt water. The shack must have had a fresh coat of white paint slapped over it just before the beginning of tourist season, Ariel judged, and wondered if the paint was holding the boards together; it certainly looked that way. A flat sheet of plywood up above the service windows had words in red paint that must have been bright not too many years back:

MARSILIO'S
GENUINE ADOCENTYN BOMBS

Nothing the counter help was handing out seemed likely to explode, however, so Ariel got into line next to Cassie. "You were about to tell me how your folks met."

That earned her a grin. "Yeah. Dad was in the army over in Korea, and some of his friends told him, hey, you got to come check out this Korean fortune teller, she's really something to see. So he let himself get talked into going. He and his friends and a bunch of other people all went into Grandma's living room and sat down on the floor, the way you do in Korea, and out comes Grandma with her bell and rattle and fan, dancing around like a wild thing and telling people she's never seen before everything about themselves. And she stops in front of my dad and says, 'The spirits say you're going to marry my youngest daughter.' Then she's off again to tell someone else's fortune."

The line lurched forward and the wind shifted, and Ariel caught the smell of Italian meat sauce and fried onions. The prospect of an Adocentyn bomb, whatever that was, started to seem more appealing.

"He got back to base that night with his friends," Cassie went on, "and of course he was thinking, no way. But he figured he ought to be polite and go visit the mudang again and explain to her why he wasn't just going to marry some random girl he's never even seen. So he goes back to the village on his next day off, and of course Grandma's expecting him even though he didn't call or anything. She waves him in and smiles and bows and has Mom come in to pour him some tea. She was cute back then, really *really* cute, I've seen photos, and he took one look and decided that maybe the spirits had a point."

They got to the front of the line. "Two bombs, totaled," Cassie said to the teenage boy behind the counter. "And two lemonades." They both handed over some cash. The teenager loaded a white paper bag with two shapes wrapped in silver paper and brought out two tall paper cups with plastic lids and straws. A few moments later Ariel had custody of both cups. Cassie took the bag and led the way over to one side of the pier, where an assortment of small round metal tables and cheap plastic chairs offered refuge impartially to the customers of half a dozen nearby food places.

One of the tables close to the sidewalk was free, with three empty chairs around it. Cassie made a beeline for it. Once they were settled, Ariel gave her one of the cups, and Cassie responded by pulling one of the objects in silver paper and handing it over. It proved to be a hot dog in a robust bun, slathered with Italian meat sauce, cheese, and a mix of fried onions, mushrooms, and peppers. Ariel took a bite, then another. "This is darb," she said. Cassie gave her a baffled look, and she translated: "Really good. Why do they call it a bomb?"

"Short for gut bomb," said Cassie. Ariel laughed, and Cassie grinned and went on: "The guys who worked at the old shipyards in South Adocentyn called it that, and it stuck."

"Okay. And what's 'totaled'?"

"With everything on it."

Ariel took another bite, decided she liked it. "You were telling me about your folks."

"Yeah. So he went out to visit her a bunch more times, he proposed, she said yes, and as soon as he got out of the army they got married and came back here. All Grandma's daughters are mudangs, it runs in the family, and so of course once Mom got settled here she started doing jeoms and kosas and kuts for the Korean people here."

"Doing what?"

"Different kinds of ceremonies. These days she does them sometimes for people who aren't Korean, too. That's Adocentyn for you."

Two cars on Harbor Street narrowly missed a fender-bender and argued about it in a flurry of blaring horns. Once the honking calmed down and both cars drove away, Ariel asked, "So are you going to be a mudang too?"

Cassie had just taken a bite of her bomb, and so was reduced to nodding enthusiastically. Once she'd swallowed, she said, "Yeah. I started learning the dances and how to make paper flowers and everything when I was five. These days I play the gong or the drum when Mom does ceremonies, and she has me do some of the ceremonies sometimes, but it's going to be a while still before my naerim kut—that's my initiation, sort of."

Ariel nodded, said nothing. Cassie watched her and then said: "You're jealous."

"Of course I am. My family doesn't do anything like that."

Cassie snorted in amusement. "No, you just have a grandfather who's one of the most famous mages in Adocentyn."

Ariel took another bite of her bomb in place of an answer. It would have been simple to point out that she was jealous of Cassie, not of Cassie's mother or grandmother, but that would have brought the conversation much too close to the perplexities that bothered her most just then. Her grandfather had spent most of his life plunging into the deep places of magic, so had Aunt Clarice, and Cassie seemed to be heading the same direction. To follow that path herself: that was the possibility that fascinated and frightened her at the same time, and after three months she was still far from sure how she was going to respond to it.

She was still trying to figure out what to say to Cassie when movement and bright color on the sidewalk caught her eye. A man dressed as a pirate was swaggering his way along the waterfront. He was in his early sixties, maybe, with a short salt-and-pepper beard framing a square weatherbeaten face. He lacked a parrot, a wooden leg, or an eyepatch, but the tricorn hat, the bright blue greatcoat, the cutlass at his side, the knee breeches and the big cuffed boots more than made up for it. He stopped in front of the table where Ariel and Cassie sat, eyed them, and said, "Arrrr!"

"Arrrr yourself," said Ariel.

Cassie choked with laughter. The pirate let out a big booming laugh, and in an ordinary voice said, "Any chance I can join you? I think you've got the only free chair in this block of Harbor Street."

Ariel and Cassie both gestured him over, and he settled onto the chair with a sigh, stretching out his feet. "Thank you," he said. "Been on my feet for hours."

"So why the pirate outfit?" Ariel asked.

"She's new in town," Cassie explained in a hurry. "I bet she's never even heard of Captain Curdie."

"Just the fish and chips place," said Ariel.

The pirate grinned. "So much for the old rascal's reputation." Then, in a proper pirate's voice: "Well, then, me beauties, let me tell ye the tale o' Captain Curdie. He was born in these parts and took to sea as a boy, as many a lad dreamed o' doing in those days, and worked his way up from cabin boy to captain of a pirate ship. The *Hawk*, that was his ship, a two-masted barquentine, the scourge of the seven seas in its day. Curdie and his crew of cutthroats plundered the Spaniards, they plundered the Dutch, if there was anybody in the world they didn't plunder, why, it was only because the scurvy dogs never got close enough to salt water.

"But in the end Curdie got tired o' the pirate life and came back to Adocentyn with his treasure, and built a house not far up the hill from here, and lived here till he died." He dropped the pirate voice. "And in 1953, I think it was, the Chamber of Commerce started hiring somebody every summer to put on pirate gear and walk up and down Harbor Avenue and say 'Arrrr!' to the tourists. The last three years, that's been me."

"You're leaving out the best part," said Cassie. "Captain Curdie's treasure. It's still around here someplace, isn't it?"

The pirate laughed yet again, a rolling laugh that got sudden startled glances from the tables around. "Don't get your hopes up," he said. "People have been looking for Captain Curdie's treasure since I don't know when. I did a little poking around myself when I was not too far from your age. I didn't find a thing and neither has anybody else."

"But it was real," Cassie insisted.

"Maybe it was. And maybe the old rascal spent every single doubloon he ever had before he died. Nobody knows. Still, far be it from me to spoil a good story, especially since it pays my rent." He hauled himself to his feet. "Well, back to work." In his pirate voice: "Thank ye, me beauties, for a safe harbor. Arrrr!"

"Arrrr," Ariel said in response, waving goodbye.

Cassie choked back another laugh, finished her bomb, and glanced at her cell phone. "Fifteen minutes," she said. "Want to head back?"

Later that afternoon, as the last bright wedge of autumn sun streamed golden through the windows of the house on Lyon

Avenue and glowed on old wallpaper and older books, she asked her grandfather about Captain Curdie.

"Yes, he was quite real." He sipped tea, set the cup down on the end table next to his armchair. "How much do you know about pirates in the American colonies?"

"Not much," Ariel admitted, sitting down on the couch facing him. "I watched a lot of bad movies when I was a kid."

That earned her a raised eyebrow, one of the few signs of amusement she'd ever seen on that impassive face. "The very short version is that the entire east coast of North America was one huge pirate haven in colonial times. Early on it was mostly privateers licensed by the British government to raid Spanish treasure fleets and merchant shipping. Later on the British stopped issuing letters of marque and reprisal—that was the proper term for a privateer's license—but by then piracy was so lucrative that nobody in the pirate trade or the colonies cared. By 1700 pirates roved the oceans of the world, seizing and plundering ships of all nations.

"Of course they had to sell the plunder and buy the supplies they needed, and the American colonies were more than willing to buy the one and sell the other. Most American historians don't like to talk about this, but a good half of the reason that the colonies flourished the way they did in the early eighteenth century is that they did so much business with pirates, fencing stolen goods and keeping the Royal Navy at arm's length. That paid off in the Revolutionary War, when the rebels filled the seven seas with privateers, who preyed on British shipping and left the British economy in shambles. That's a good half of why the British finally gave up and made peace."

Ariel nodded, taking this in.

"As for Bartholomew Curdie, he was one of the more successful pirates of his time. He was Scottish by ancestry but he was born not far from here in 1686, I think it was, and went to sea as a boy of eight. By the time he was thirty he'd worked his way up to first mate of a merchant ship, but he wasn't satisfied with that, so he took ship with the pirate captain Calico Jack Rackham. He did well enough out of it that in 1721 he bought his own ship, the *Hawk*, and sailed away under the Jolly Roger. He went all over the world, but every few years he'd come back here, drop anchor in Coopers Bay, and spend a few months on land while the *Hawk* was being refitted and his crew spent their money—" He allowed a fractional shrug. "There's no other way to put it: like drunken sailors.

"In 1731, though, he came back to stay. He'd had a hard fight with the Royal Navy off the Lesser Antilles, and though he got away he lost nearly half his crew and he'd taken some serious wounds himself. So the *Hawk* limped into port and he kissed the ground and swore that he'd never set foot on a ship's deck again. It turned out he'd bought quite a bit of land here on his previous visits, and so he built a house on what was then still farmland east of town, settled down, and spent the rest of his life here. He died in 1758, and you can see his tomb in St. Cyprian's church downtown if you like."

Ariel nodded again. "Was there actually a treasure?"

"Nobody knows." He sipped tea. "Doubtless Curdie had plenty of it when he came back from his last voyage. He'd circled the world again, raided a Mughal treasure fleet in the Indian Ocean, and caught a couple of Spanish galleons loaded with gold while they were napping off the Philippines. But he spent money very freely once he was ashore. He helped pay for the first library in town, contributed quite a bit to the building of St. Cyprian's, and so on. After he died, there were rumors, but his house was one of the ones that burnt down when the British shelled Adocentyn during the War of 1812, and nowadays nobody knows where it was."

Ariel gave him a puzzled look. "Nobody knows? Wasn't there a foundation, or a cellar, or something like that?"

"Too many of them. Curdie bought a good-sized piece of the land between the edge of the old town and Lambspring Point, and as the town grew, he sold it off in pieces, a block here, two blocks there. This house is built on part of his estate, for example. By 1812 around half the estate was already built up, and Curdie's house was part of a neighborhood. No doubt people at the time remembered which house was his, but after the rebuilding, nobody happened to write that detail down. Based on what I've read, quite a few of the new houses were rebuilt on old foundations. It's quite possible that one of them is his, but which one? People have been trying to figure that out for more than a century now."

A sudden improbable thought leapt up in Ariel's mind. Before she could speak, Dr. Moravec raised a finger. "You're wondering whether this house might be the one."

"Well, yes," she admitted.

"I'm sorry to disappoint you, but it isn't. This neighborhood wasn't built up until Culpeper Park was laid out in 1869. There were a few farmhouses nearby before then, but I had a specialist in to look at the foundation and it's late nineteenth century work."

"You had a specialist in," said Ariel. With a grin: "Because you wanted to find it."

Dr. Moravec shrugged. "A chest full of pirate treasure would have made it much easier to afford some of the books I had my eye on back then," he admitted. "But I didn't seriously expect to find the treasure, even if this house turned out to be built on Curdie's foundations. People have been hunting for Captain Curdie's treasure since the 1850s, and this neighborhood has seen quite a bit of searching. When I bought this house there were still signs that someone had been digging holes in the ground in the backyard."

She nodded, fell silent for a little while. The old man regarded her with a calm uncommunicative gaze. Finally she said, "You know, you haven't asked me how the classes with Aunt Clarice are going yet."

"I assumed you would tell me when you were ready," he replied, imperturbable as ever. "How are they going?"

"I'm not sure." She made a little shrug. "I know a lot more about St. John's wort than I thought there was to know. I know how to garble herbs and how to grind them in a mortar and pestle. I'm not sure how much that has to do with magic, but I'll keep at it."

Dr. Moravec nodded. "Good. The thing to keep in mind is that what you can see is the least important part of magic. The part that matters is the work that goes on inside the mind, the heart—" A gesture reached for the indescribable. "The consciousness of the mage. That's something you have to learn a little at a time."

Ariel considered that. "Can't you just explain it?"

"I wish." He picked up his teacup again, sipped from it. "To practice magic, you have to understand the world the way mages do, and that doesn't come naturally in this age of the world. The book by Eliphas Lévi I gave you teaches the great secrets of magic more clearly than I could. Have you started it?"

"I skimmed a little," she admitted. "It didn't make a lot of sense to me."

"Of course not. It didn't make much sense to me the first time I read it, either. The second reading teaches a little more, the third more still, and a year or two from now you'll slap your head and wonder how you missed so much. In the meantime, you're starting to learn certain practical skills that will help you a great deal in investigations, and if you decide you want to learn more, they'll help you even more then. I know that it's a slow process, but—" He shrugged. "That's the way of it."

She made a tentative nod. "Like putting together clues to a mystery."

"A little like that, yes." He sipped tea again. "That reminds me. I've made progress on the current case. I've got inquiries out at the booksellers. Nothing yet, but they're watching for any book like the one the Kozlowskis lost. Also, while you were at class, Father Novak called. What's your schedule this week?"

"Aunt Clarice won't have any time free to teach until next Monday. I've called Jill about helping with the horses Thursday, but I can call her back and reschedule if I have to."

"That won't be necessary. He's agreed to meet me tomorrow at ten."

"Berries," said Ariel, grinning. "Count me in."

CHAPTER 4

A QUESTION OF EVIL

When she'd starting assisting her grandfather in his investigations, Ariel had taken on certain duties, and one of them involved going through the morning edition of the *Adocentyn Mercury* every day to clip out articles of interest. Dr. Moravec got the print edition of the paper, tossed onto the doorstep each morning near dawn by a plump middle-aged woman named Ms. Pawelik. Each morning, right after downing her first cup of coffee and a couple of pieces of toast, Ariel spread the paper out on the dining table and perched on a chair with scissors and a list of topics in her grandfather's neat handwriting close by.

The day after her encounter with the pirate and her first Adocentyn bomb was typical. The day was clear and bright, and sun streamed in through the kitchen window to pool on the linoleum floor and the battered old table where she'd put the paper. The phone rang. She tensed, and then reminded herself that it wasn't Saturday and so it wouldn't be her mother calling. It turned out to be a robot call about her auto warranty. Since she didn't own a car, and her grandfather's Buick was so old that she suspected its warranty was on display somewhere in a museum of fossils, she rolled her eyes and hung up on the recording before the machine had gotten through its first sentence.

Returning to the table, she wrinkled her nose at the smell of fresh newsprint and skipped the front page, well stocked as usual with the latest bleak news from elsewhere in the world. The local section further in was her goal. Two stories about the Heydonian Institution, the centuries-old library and museum of magical lore just east of Adocentyn's downtown, started the day's pile of clippings. One of the mansions in the old-money neighborhood near the Heydonian was being put up for sale, and that story joined the pile; so did a few column inches several pages later about a building project in the oldest part of downtown.

The police blotter page—the *Mercury* still had that venerable feature in its local news section—reported a daytime burglary in the Culpeper Hill neighborhood, no suspects, no witnesses. The scissors made their harsh whisper and freed the story from the rest of the paper. Down at the bottom of the page was a brief notice about the prowler Cassie and Aunt Clarice mentioned. Ariel considered that. It wasn't one of the things on her grandfather's list, but she cut it out anyway, set it aside for future reference.

The door of Dr. Moravec's study was open, so Ariel took the clippings straight in and set them on the corner of his desk. He was settled in an easy chair in one corner of the study, all his attention on a big leatherbound book with a Latin title in faded gold leaf, and he showed no signs of noticing her existence. It occurred to her, glancing at him, that he spent much more time studying magic than she did, even though she was a raw beginner and he was a trustee of the Heydonian Institution. That dampened her mood: was magic that hard to understand?

The rest of the newspaper went into a stack next to the recycle bin, where it would stay for a few weeks in case there was some reason to read it again, and soap and water from the sink got the newsprint off her hands. Once that was taken care of, she got another cup of coffee and settled on the parlor sofa with her French dictionary and the book by Eliphas Lévi.

The title, *Dogme et Rituel de la Haute Magie*, translated out as *Doctrine and Ritual of High Magic*. That sounded promising, but the introduction was written in lurid nineteenth-century prose and seemed to be about everything but how to cast a spell. *A travers le voile de toutes les allegories hiératiques et mystiques*, it began, and she interpreted that easily enough: *Beyond the veil of all hieratic and mystic allegories*. She rolled her eyes, made herself keep reading.

An hour passed, maybe, before her grandfather unfolded himself from his chair and came into the parlor. "Ready?"

She set aside the volume of Lévi, trying to suppress a sigh of relief. "Let me grab my shoulder bag," she said, and trotted past him to the stairs.

Moments later, as billowing white clouds towered above Culpeper Hill and a scattering of orange and yellow leaves blew past from the park, Ariel climbed behind the wheel of the Buick. She slung the shoulder bag into a convenient place, pulled the door shut and waited for Dr. Moravec to settle into the passenger seat. "Where to?"

"Ivy to Hazel," the old man said. "Left on Hazel, and keep going. I'll explain the rest once we get closer."

The engine turned over, settled into a throaty purr. She pulled away from the curb and slid the Buick into the sparse afternoon traffic. "Anything I need to know about Father Novak?"

"Not much. He knows a little about my work, though of course he disapproves of it, and we've worked together a few times. He's always been cordial. Of course the first time we met, I happened to introduce him to the woman he married."

She sent a puzzled glance his way. "I thought he was a Catholic priest."

"Not that kind of Catholic." After a moment, when her baffled look hadn't changed: "The Roman Church is the largest Catholic denomination but it's far from the only one. Father Novak is with the Polish National Catholic Church, which split from the Roman Church in the nineteenth century. They have churches all over the east coast and the Midwest, St. Adalbert's is their parish here, and yes, their priests can marry."

She turned onto Ivy Street, where houses two centuries old gave way to a pleasant little commercial strip. The traffic thickened—Ivy was one of the main routes through the upper end of the Culpeper Hill neighborhood—and she concentrated on driving. The left turn onto Hazel didn't help matters much, since Hazel was the first street across town east of Culpeper Park and was nearly as busy as Ivy. It wasn't until they'd gone past the park and the great oaks gave way to a neighborhood of sprawling Victorian mansions that Ariel could spare any attention from the traffic. Right about then Dr. Moravec said, "Six more blocks, and then right on Garibaldi and look for a parking place."

On the far side of the mansion district were less impressive houses of the same vintage, and then a little business district with Garibaldi Street running through the middle of it. Ariel made the turn, found a space without too much difficulty, and parked two buildings short of a modestly sized brick church a century old, with a few missing tiles on the roof and a general air of mild dilapidation. It had two signs out front, rising out of the lawn on wooden posts. One read CHURCH OF ST. ADALBERT P.N.C.C.; the other, close to the main door, had a painted thermometer on it, announcing the progress of the latest drive to boost the maintenance fund. The red bar hadn't risen very far yet.

Ariel got out of the Buick, waited for her grandfather to do the same, and then followed him past the church to a brick house next to it with a smaller sign out front that read RECTORY. They climbed three steps to the porch, Dr. Moravec knocked on the door, and after a discreet interval the lock rattled and a middle-aged man opened it. His black clothing and the little white square of the collar under his chin were wholly unnecessary, Ariel thought, because nobody could have looked more like a clergyman than he did: thin and stoop-shouldered, clean-shaven, black hair with just a little gray at the temples, hard lines etched around his mouth and eyes by most of a life-time's worth of disappointed optimism. He beamed at the two of them, and his smile was just as clerical as the rest of him, at once genial and a little embarrassed.

"Good morning, Bernard," he said. "And—I don't believe we've met."

"My assistant Ariel Moravec," said Dr. Moravec. "Ariel, Father Vincent Novak."

The priest shook her hand. "Very pleased to meet you. If I had to guess, I'd say you chose an assistant among your rela-tives. Please, come in."

"Yes," said Dr. Moravec as they stepped into the entry. "Ariel's also my granddaughter. I hadn't expected my line of work to run in the family, but—" A shrug punctuated the sentence.

"Why, neither did I." The priest's smile brightened a little as they reached the parlor, which was small and dowdy but very clean. All the furniture had been old before Ariel was born. Windows looking out over rose bushes still in flower let in a splash of color and sunlight.

"Ah. Your son?"

"Began classes at the seminary in Scranton a few days ago. It's costing us a good bit of money, of course, but we're all very proud of him." He motioned them toward a sofa. "Would either of you like coffee?"

That and some aimless conversation about the priest's son took up a few minutes. His wife Agnieszka, who was brown-haired and plump and wore a slightly shabby blue dress with a high neckline, took up a few more; she brought the coffee out, greeted Dr. Moravec with a fixed smile that didn't do much to hide her obvious discomfort, pressed Ariel's hand with less reluctance but an uncertain look. Finally, though, Agnieszka went somewhere else, Father Vincent perched on the front edge of a chair, Dr. Moravec settled more comfortably into one corner of the sofa, and Ariel sat in the other and got out her notebook and a pen.

"The Kozlowski book," said Father Vincent then. "Of course I know about it, though under other circumstances I wouldn't discuss that knowledge."

"I appreciate that you're willing to do so," said Dr. Moravec.

"Oh, I talked to Teresa first, and she told me that I should tell you everything she's passed on to me. She's very concerned about what might be done with that book. She was devout even before her husband passed away, and since then—" He gestured. "You know how it is. The last time she missed Sunday Mass was when little Joseph had infected tonsils, and that was two years ago. She helps out with the altar guild when she can, though that's not often. She doesn't have much free time, between work and her family."

Dr. Moravec nodded, said nothing.

"But she told me about the book not long after I became pastor here. She's always been very uncomfortable about having it at all. I'm sure she would have gotten rid of it, probably by way of the fireplace, if she hadn't made a promise to her grandmother. But I asked her to bring it here, and of course she did."

"I'm curious what you made of it," said Dr. Moravec.

"If I were more of a Latin scholar I might have something to tell you." A rueful shrug and a shake of his head emphasized the point. "A Latin manuscript in late medieval black letter is beyond me. The family tradition was that it's a book of magic, and it certainly might be. It has diagrams in it of circles with words written around them. That's your specialty and not mine, but they looked like circles for conjuring spirits."

"How many diagrams?"

The priest thought for a moment. "At least half a dozen. Maybe nine or ten, but I don't think it was quite so many as that."

Dr. Moravec nodded and said nothing.

"I advised her to keep it someplace where the children couldn't get at it, and leave it alone. As far as I know, that's exactly what she did. I didn't think about it again until she called me to let me know that somebody had stolen it."

"And the whole conversation was under the seal of the confessional?"

"Yes. We're still quite strict about that, of course."

"I'm glad to hear it. The fewer people know about the book, the more chance there is of identifying the thief."

Father Vincent allowed a smile. "Oh, granted. I think of it in less pragmatic terms."

"If you didn't," said Dr. Moravec, "I'd be concerned. One other question comes to mind. Do you happen to know whether Ms. Kozlowski mentioned the book to anyone else?"

"Not to my knowledge, no. I don't imagine she would, though."

A little conversation about mutual friends rounded off the visit. Dr. Moravec stood, then, and Ariel did the same thing a heartbeat later. Hands got shaken, pleasantries said, and then she followed her grandfather out into the autumn sunlight.

The drive home was uneventful, the rest of the day not much different, with an hour or so spent struggling through the rest of Lévi's introduction its most noticeable feature. The next morning brought another newspaper and a few more articles of interest, including one about the prowler; Ariel clipped it out and took it upstairs to her desk to join the one from the day before.

She had other things on her mind that morning, though, because her new home and her new job as her grandfather's assistant hadn't been the only unexpected results of her first investigation. She'd also ended up making a friend of one of the clients, who kept a boarding stable outside the little town of Criswell a dozen miles west of town. The friendship came with riding privileges: that was how Ariel thought of it, though it was just as true that five horses whose owners only got out to see them on the weekends needed plenty of exercise and a spare rider was always welcome, even if she wasn't exactly an expert equestrienne.

By eight that morning, accordingly, she was at the transit mall downtown, in the shadow of both of Adocentyn's biggest skyscrapers, waiting for the 38 bus to Criswell. Before nine she was saying good morning to Jill Callahan, who owned the farm with her husband Ben; to Ricky Higgins, who lived in a cottage in back and ran the stable; and to the horses, who had long since gotten used to her weekly visits. Riding clothes from her shoulder bag and a hard day on horseback duly followed.

When she boarded the bus a little after three o'clock for the trip back home, every muscle from her shoulders down was explaining to her in strident tones just how much work it had put in that day. None of them was much less vocal by the time she got back to the transit mall. The thought of what they'd say to her if she walked home from there was unwelcome enough that she crossed the mall to a different stop, where she could catch the next route 9 bus along Ivy Street and get off two blocks from home. Two of the other people waiting at that stop looked vaguely familiar when she started across, but it wasn't until she was most of the way there that she realized that it was Teresa Kozlowski and her daughter Lucy. The battered but well-stuffed canvas bags they carried suggested a successful shopping trip.

"Hi," Lucy said, as soon as Ariel got within speaking range. "You're the detective, right?"

"No, just the detective's assistant. Hi, Lucy. And— Ms. Kozlowski, right?"

"Teresa." Lucy's mother looked tired but put on a smile. "Hi."

"I hope everything's okay," said Ariel.

"More or less. Paul's doing better than usual today, so he's babysitting Joey while Lucy and I do some shopping."

"Mom picked me up right when school let out," said Lucy, "and we took two buses to the big thrift store out on West Main. You've gone there, right?"

"Not yet," said Ariel. "I'm kind of new in town, and I haven't had time to go looking for the good thrift stores."

Teresa's face brightened a little. "You might try the Ivy Street Thrift Emporium," she said. "It's the one I go to most often. Three blocks from where I live, on the corner of Ivy and Holly. It's pretty good."

"You can find all kinds of stuff there," said Lucy. "Clothes and toys and everything."

"I'll try it," said Ariel. "Thanks."

"Sometime when you're not detecting," Lucy said, and then, with a sudden grin: "So what can you detect about me?"

Ariel gave the child a wry look, and said in her best fake Sherlock Holmes accent, "I deduce that you've grown two inches since your mom bought those pants for you."

Lucy giggled. "Yeah, but that's easy."

"And I deduce," Ariel went on, "that you think Princess Panda is the best thing ever."

Lucy's mouth fell open. Behind her, Teresa put a hand to her mouth to stifle a laugh. "Okay," said Lucy. "How did you know?"

"Elementary, my dear Lucy," said Ariel, getting another giggle. "Look at your wrist."

Lucy did, and turned pink. Faded but still visible, a rub-on temporary tattoo showed the cartoon character, complete with crown and pink ballerina tutu.

"You're tope," Lucy said, with an admiring look. "I wanted the Magic Sign but Mom says those books are really bad."

"You know what?" said Ariel. "Your mom is right."

Teresa mouthed the words "thank you" silently.

The bus pulled up then. Most of the seats were already taken but a side-facing bench seat in back was still empty. The three of them got settled on it while the bus lurched forward and began winding its way through the streets of downtown Adocentyn. Teresa leaned toward Ariel. In a low voice: "I hope you and Dr. Moravec can find that book. I hate to think what might happen if somebody tries to do something with it."

"Dr. Moravec thinks he has some leads," Ariel told her.

"Oh, thank God," Teresa said. The look of relief seemed genuine enough. "If there's anything else I can do to help, please have him give me a call."

"I'll let him know," said Ariel, with what she hoped was a reassuring smile.

More people got on at the next stop, and still more at the one after that. By the time the bus got close to Ariel's stop it was all she could do to say a quick goodbye to Teresa and Lucy and squeeze through the crowd to the back door. Once she was safely out on the sidewalk and the bus grumbled to itself and rolled on, Ariel drew a deep breath and started up Lyon Avenue toward her grandfather's house.

What circled through her thoughts as she walked was Lucy's comment about the Magic Sign. That was from the Bertie Scrubb books, of course, one detail out of the mass of fake magic that filled those heavily marketed volumes of children's fiction. "Really bad" was the way Ariel liked to describe the series, too, but she knew their literary quality wasn't what Teresa Kozlowski had in mind.

Evil, she thought as she neared the old house. There were people who thought that all magic was evil, just as there were people who thought that all magic was empty superstition. She'd met people in both categories often enough before. It was easy enough for her to ignore the self-proclaimed skeptics—even before she'd moved to Adocentyn and started working for her grandfather, she'd seen things that no argument could explain away—but the other set of claims troubled her.

Memory brought up the face of Olive Kellinger, the witch of Criswell, who'd blighted dozens of lives with her curses and who'd tried to kill Ariel with a spell when she'd finally been unmasked. That brought up more memories, the harsh magic Dr. Moravec had used to break her power, the simpler but equally harsh charm for the same purpose Ariel had learned from Aunt Clarice. Behind them all hovered a memory from Ariel's childhood, a weeping ghost at the water's edge in evening twilight, who only appeared when others were about to die. All of it felt too close to evil for her comfort.

Troubled, she resolved to ask her grandfather about the subject sometime, and forced her thoughts clear. Another block brought her to the familiar green house with the oaks of Culpeper Park beyond them. The familiar sound of the front door shutting behind her didn't quite succeed in shutting out her thoughts, but it came close. Her grandfather was busy in his study, and the door was shut: meditating, she guessed, or doing another practice he hadn't explained to her yet. She went upstairs, put her riding clothes into the hamper, and headed back down to the parlor.

As she got there, the study door opened and her grandfather looked out. "Ariel? Good afternoon. May I ask what your plans are tomorrow?"

"I didn't have any," she admitted. "What's up?"

"I need a note to get to a bookstore downtown, and I don't expect to have the spare time to take it there myself."

"How early?"

His gesture dismissed the question. "Whenever's convenient."

"Duck soup. Just give me directions—I don't know downtown that well yet."

"I'll have it in writing for you tomorrow." Then, before she could ask him about her worries, he was back inside the study and the door clicked shut.

A cup of hot tea offered some solace. So did the least visible decoration in the parlor, a little black wooden crocodile perched atop one of the tall bookcases, its toothy mouth open, gazing down as though contemplating its next victim. She grinned up at it, settled down on the sofa, and picked up Lévi's book.

Downtown, she thought. Cassie said the library had lots of old books—and I might be able to find out where Captain Curdie's estate was.

The book in her hand reminded her that she had something else to think about. She opened it, found her place, and began to wrestle with the French. *When a philosopher took for the base of a new revelation of human wisdom ...* That was how the first chapter began, and the connection between the rest of the paragraph and magic still eluded her. She sighed, sipped coffee, and kept reading.

CHAPTER 5

A HOUSE OF GHOSTS

The bookstore looked as though it hadn't opened its doors during Ariel's lifetime. A storefront in a sprawling red brick commercial building of early nineteenth-century vintage, with faded signage up above the entrance reading DUPOIS & CO. ANTIQUE BOOKSELLERS, it had tall windows on either side of the door and an oval window in the door itself, but a gate of welded iron bars closed the doorway off and the windows had more bars fencing them in. No lights showed from inside. It took Ariel most of a minute to spot the little note on faded paper just inside one window: *Open at 2pm today*.

A jaundiced look at the note, and another at the barricaded door, didn't alter the situation, and it didn't help that the ink on the note looked faded. She found herself wondering which day "today" meant, and if it belonged to that decade or some more distant era. A glance at her watch, another thrift store find, confirmed that at best, she had two hours to wait. She turned, called to mind what Cassie had said about the downtown library, and tried to guess how to find it.

Around her, downtown Adocentyn climbed skyward from streets full of traffic to roofs and cornices loaded down with the soot-stained decor of three centuries. The building with the bookstore had carved lions on the cornice three stories up, gazing down with open mouths as though the spectacle below

45

astonished them. The one behind her lacked faces of any kind peering out from its walls but made up for it with fake Greek pillars between each of the storefronts and a parade of vaguely classical figures carved in a band of once-white stone above that, marching gamely from one end of the building to the other. Art Deco skyscrapers loomed over all, each with its own improbable ornaments. Just past the corner at the end of that block, for that matter, she could glimpse a little of a building of dark stone, and it had a genuine bat-winged gargoyle looming out from the roofline.

That intrigued Ariel, and she went toward it. From the corner itself she could see the whole structure, a big stone church in the Gothic style. It looked as though some unknown force had torn a medieval English abbey church out of the ground in a single piece, hauled it across the ocean, and set it down with unexpected gentleness on the first convenient vacant lot. It had an abundance of gargoyles along the edge of the roof and nearly as many stained glass windows in pointed Gothic arches below. Ariel wondered what it was like inside, but had almost decided to turn away and go looking for the library when she noticed the sign mounted on the wall below the gargoyle: St. Cyprian's Church.

She paused, pulled a notebook from her purse, flipped through a few pages to make sure she'd remembered correctly, then darted across the street as soon as the traffic allowed and set out to find a door. Discreet signs pointed her the right way. The door itself had a demure little sign of its own, listing hours that, to her surprise, included that day and time. She tried the door, found that it opened smoothly, and went through into the shadows of the vestibule and then into the great echoing nave of the church.

She'd seen photos and videos of the insides of medieval Gothic churches before. This one could have passed for any of them: soaring vertical lines rising to the high arches of the ceiling, fluted pillars topped with ornate carvings, sunlight through stained glass splashing color across dark wooden pews and the darker stone of the floor, dim shapes in the shadows ahead gradually turning into a high altar surrounded by an altar rail as she came closer. The hush inside the church surprised her with its intensity: as though she could shout aloud, she thought, and not trouble the silence in the least.

She had just started searching the floor and the walls for the thing she wanted to find when the shadows near her gathered together into a human shape and said in a dry soft voice, "Perhaps I can help you find something."

"Please," Ariel said, glancing up in surprise. An old woman in a dowdy black dress stood nearby. Her face was almost as pale as her bone-white hair, and her hands made two additional spots of white against the dress. It took a second glance for Ariel to notice that the dress had the little white square of a clerical collar at the throat.

"I'm looking for the grave of Captain Curdie. I heard from someone that it's in here."

"It is indeed." The old woman motioned and started walking, and Ariel followed. The dark gray flagstones under their feet had long rectangles of pale stone set into them, and Ariel realized with a flicker of discomfort that she was walking over the dead.

"The old reprobate hardly belongs in sacred ground," said the old woman as they walked. "But he donated quite a bit of money to build the old church, the one that this replaced. Buying your way into heaven, no, you can't do that, but into a church? I'm sorry to say it happens all the time." She glanced over her shoulder, kept walking. "Tell me this. Are you by any chance hoping to find the treasure?"

"Well, maybe," Ariel said. "I'm just curious, mostly. I know a lot of people have gone looking for it already."

"Oh, yes. That was already going on long before I was a little girl." She laughed, a soft dry sound like falling sand. "A few years ago now. But I was just out of school when Delphinia

Braddock published her book, and that sent many more people after it." A few more steps and she slowed, moved to one side. "Ah, here we are. The most popular tomb we have. I suppose having a genuine pirate buried in one's church has a certain cachet."

The white stone in the floor differed only in detail from the other memorial stones in the church, a pale rectangle of marble about the size of the coffin beneath it. The words carved into it were still legible despite three centuries of shuffling feet:

CAPT · BART^W · CURDIE

BORN 1686 DYED 1758

S · Y · S · B · I · Y · C

A silent minute or two passed. "Does anyone know what the letters down below mean?" Ariel asked. "I don't think I've seen them on a grave before."

The old woman allowed a little smile. "No, and you won't see them on any other. The story is that when Curdie was dying, he had one of his servants write those letters down, and told him to have them carved on his tomb. Those are supposed to be the one and only clue to where he hid the treasures he brought back from his voyages. Is that true or not? I have no idea. He's not one of the ones who walks here at night, so I haven't asked him."

Ariel glanced up sharply from the stone. "Walks," she said. "You mean ghosts?"

"Why, yes, of course. The ghosts of St. Cyprian's are practically famous. We've had writers and researchers coming here for years."

"I didn't know," Ariel admitted. "I've only been in Adocentyn for three months."

The old woman considered her, and then nodded. "Ah. Between that and your face, I might be able to guess your family name, then. Would it be Moravec?"

"You know my grandfather," said Ariel.

"Of course. By John Heydon's original bequest, the minister of St. Cyprian's is always a trustee of the Heydonian Institution. That's who I am, of course." She reached out a hand. "Margaret Hynd. You can put 'reverend' in front of that if you must, but I'd rather you didn't."

"Ariel Moravec," said Ariel, pressing the hand. Cold, thin, and dry, it felt like a bundle of twigs.

"Very pleased to make your acquaintance. Since you came to town so recently, I'm going to guess you haven't read much about the treasure."

"I only heard about it a few days ago."

"Well, there you are. If you're interested, you should certainly read Braddock's book. It gets reprinted every few years, and they have plenty of copies at the downtown branch of the library, just a few blocks from here. It's hardly even out of your way."

"I was planning on going there," Ariel admitted. "If you could tell me the title—"

The minister smiled again: the same little smile, veiling secrets. "Of course." She waited while Ariel got a notebook out of her shoulder bag, and then said, "*Captain Curdie's Treasure* by Delphinia Braddock." She spelled the first name. Then, with the smile unchanged: "Please give my best regards to your grandfather. We've had some mild differences of opinion at times, so he may find that a little unexpected, but tell him anyway."

Ariel nodded, finished copying down the title and author of the book, and added a copy of the writing on the gravestone for good measure. "I'll tell him," she said. An old memory edged with dread surfaced in her thoughts. "The ghosts here— do they ever hurt anybody?"

The old woman looked shocked. "Good heavens, no. They're very well behaved. If they gave anyone the least trouble I'd have some words with them, and they wouldn't like that at all." Her shoulders moved up fractionally in a little shrug. "I have to do exorcisms from time to time, of course, but I can't imagine I'd ever have to do one here in the church."

Ariel gave her an uneasy look. The old woman smiled again, and motioned to one side of the church. "If you go that way, you'll leave by the north door, and that will put you just three blocks from the library. Up Seventh Avenue, then turn the corner onto Commerce Street and you can't miss it. That and the Heydonian are the only buildings in town that rival this one. Well, then. Good afternoon, Ariel."

"Good afternoon," Ariel said, and went toward the north door as she'd been directed. After a few steps she glanced back, but the Reverend Margaret Hynd had vanished into the shadows again. Ariel turned away and hurried to the door.

The traffic noise, cloud-tattered sunlight, and half-familiar buildings on Seventh Avenue offered some relief. Only when she'd reached the sidewalk did Ariel let herself wonder if she'd spoken to a living person or a ghost. The question had no obvious answer; the one ghost she knew she'd seen, many years back, had looked and sounded like a living person, and only a terrible sense of wrongness gathering about that small shape in the evening light had warned her. Not all ghosts gave off the same impression: she knew that, too.

The street ahead gave her something else to think about. When she reached the corner of Seventh and Commerce, the downtown branch of the Adocentyn Public Library did the same thing, and then some. It rose up in front of her in all its glory, an Egyptian Revival hallucination in sand-colored stone. Two great sphinxes guarded the Commerce Street entrance, glowering at the traffic through half-lidded eyes. Behind them, flanked by two soaring statues of hawk-headed gods, huge bronze doors stood open, revealing glass doors on a merely human scale within. The wall facing the street rose sheer, pierced here and there by narrow windows in pairs, to a cornice carved with stylized lotus leaves. The merely commercial buildings that flanked the library seemed to edge away from it, as though they didn't want to risk a pharaoh's wrath.

Ariel blinked, shook herself, and kept walking toward it. Improbably, it didn't dissolve into something less gaudy as she approached. She passed the sphinxes, crossed the flagstoned porch between the two statues, reached the glass doors, and passed through them into a perfectly ordinary public library with a checkout desk on the left, a new book display on the right featuring the latest Bertie Scrubb novel among others, and tan-colored steel shelves loaded with books reaching away into the middle distance in the glare of fluorescent lights. Only the carpet, lapis lazuli blue with a pattern of gold hieroglyphics on it, did anything to soften the transition.

The biggest library Ariel had ever visited before then was a third the size or less, but it took her only a few moments to get her bearings, locate a map, and find the escalator. That took her to the third floor, where the map showed books on history. The shelves around her had Dewey decimal numbers in the 900s on them, confirming it. A computer kiosk not far from the escalator was emblazoned with the words LIBRARY CATALOG, conveniently enough; a minute there and a few minutes weaving through shelves stuffed to the bursting point with books, and she pulled down a new edition of *Captain Curdie's Treasure* by Delphinia Braddock from its place between two other recent volumes on local history. The painted pirate on the glossy cover even looked a little like the man she'd met on the waterfront.

That amused her, but she hadn't forgotten her original plan. A glance around the third floor didn't offer any guidance. Fortunately the big desk marked INFORMATION had a librarian seated behind it, typing on a keyboard in a listless way that suggested she was waiting for something more interesting to do.

"Why, of course I can," said the librarian, a stocky black woman in a light blue jacket and skirt, with silver-framed bifocals perched low on her nose and a necklace of ornate silver beads tracing multiple arcs across her white silk blouse. "You come right this way." She led Ariel through a gap in the stacks to an alcove, where atlases and volumes of maps too tall for ordinary shelves lay flat on broad shelves on their own, and big sturdy tables waited for them.

The volume Ariel needed, a record of the city's plats, was nearly the size of a small tabletop itself. The librarian took one end, Ariel took the other, and they carried it to one of the tables. There the librarian opened it and turned half a dozen thick cream-colored pages. "Now why don't you tell me what part of town you're looking for," the librarian said then.

"The part that used to be Captain Bartholomew Curdie's property," said Ariel.

That earned her a big bright smile. "Looking for his treasure?"

"I thought I'd give it a try," Ariel said. "Do you get a lot of people asking about that?"

"Well, not that often, but two or three times a year there's somebody, and this floor of the library is where they usually come first." The librarian turned a few more pages. "Here you go. Now when you get done with this, if you need help getting it back where it belongs, you come get me, okay?" Ariel promised she would, and the librarian headed back to her desk.

The page in front of Ariel showed a half-familiar landscape mapped out in the precise draftsmanship of an earlier century. Lambspring Point, not yet graced with its lighthouse, reached nearly to one edge of the page. The north shore of Coopers Bay ran along the bottom of the page from there to the halfway mark and the Shetamunk River took it from there. North of the bay and the river, colonial Adocentyn climbed the slope from the water's edge to the hills. Downtown was a striped fabric of long thin landholdings that ran north from narrow footholds on the river, already divided by streets with familiar names. East of there, not quite touching the mouth of the river, was

John Heydon's farm, where the Heydonian Institution would rise a century later; past that were two other farms, and then—

Ariel's breath caught. A big rectangle of land between Coopers Bay and the oak woods that would become Culpeper Park was marked BART. CURDIE ESTATE. The map didn't show buildings, and apparently none of the streets of the Culpeper Hill neighborhood had yet been platted out. She frowned, turned a dozen more pages, and found another map of that part of town showing the streets as they had been set out after the British bombardment in 1814.

That map had a scale divided in hundred-yard segments. So did the one showing the Curdie estate. It took Ariel only a moment and a sheet of paper from the notebook in her shoulder bag to copy both scales. A few minutes of flipping from page to page let her work out which streets had been built on the old pirate's property. Her pen darted across the notebook, jotting down the crucial details: Curdie's estate covered the ground from Crown Street south to the harbor, and from Oak Avenue east to Holly Avenue: sixty blocks in all, including nearly half of the Culpeper Hill neighborhood and the old waterfront at its foot. That stirred something in the back of her mind, and she stood there for a little while, frowning, trying to coax whatever it was to the surface.

The effort didn't accomplish anything, so she gave the maps another close look, then shut the book and got it back onto its shelf without too much difficulty. A glance at the big clock up on the wall near the escalators told Ariel that she still had most of an hour before the odd little bookstore opened. She considered her options, went past the librarian's desk again, thanked her, and then rode the escalator further up.

The Unpopular Literature section, Ariel thought when she reached the fourth floor: the label Cassie had given it certainly seemed to fit. Long lines of shelves packed with old books stretched away beneath the fluorescent lamps like headstones in a well-ordered graveyard, and a genuine wooden card catalog up against one wall promised to tell where the bodies were buried. Most of the late deceased were novels, she guessed, but not all; Dewey decimal numbers on the ends of the shelves showed where nonfiction books could be found. She paused, then glanced at the spine of the book by Delphinia Braddock and went looking for the same number.

It took her a little while to find it, and when she did she was annoyed to discover that the books in question were on the topmost shelf, out of her reach. A few more minutes went into looking for some way to remedy that. Finally, perched atop a slightly rickety three-step ladder, she got close enough to see the titles on the shelf. There were two older editions of Delphinia Braddock's book, as she'd guessed, but next to those was another volume, shorter but considerably thicker. Like all the books in that section, it had the kind of slick cloth binding libraries used most of a century before, with an abbreviated version of the title, the author's last name, and the Dewey decimal number stamped on the spine.

Intrigued, she pulled CAPT. CURDIE WEMBERLY out of its place, climbed down from the ladder, and opened it. The title page, yellowed with the years, told her that the title was *The Treasure of Captain Curdie, A Colonial Enigma*, the author was one Maude Gorton Wemberly, and the book had been published in 1889. A glance at the table of contents showed that it was partly about Curdie's life but mostly about his treasure, and it was nearly twice as long as Delphinia Braddock's book. Ariel spent a moment flipping through the pages, stopped at an unexpected glimpse of white.

Somebody had marked a place in the book by tearing off a small piece from a sheet of paper and putting it in between two pages. A dozen pages further on, there was another, and then more: seven in all. Four of them were plain blank paper, but the other three had little black marks on one edge, as though they'd been torn from something that had print on it.

Ariel closed the book and tucked it under her arm with the one by Delphinia Braddock. The clock on the wall by the escalators showed quarter to two. The old novels would have to wait, she decided, and headed for the checkout desk on the ground floor.

Checking out the books took her a few minutes longer than she expected. The one by Braddock was simple enough—the librarian scanned a bar code inside the front cover, and that was the end of it—but the one by Wemberly from the fourth floor didn't have a bar code. The librarian had to type something on his computer keyboard and then wait for something else to appear on the screen. It was only because of the delay that she happened to be looking at the main doors, for want of anything better to do.

That was why she spotted a half-familiar figure dressed in black clerical clothing as he came through one of the doors. It took her a moment to recognize Father Vincent Novak. He seemed preoccupied, and hurried past the checkout desk without noticing Ariel. As she watched, he went straight to the escalator and rode it up out of sight.

CHAPTER 6

AN UNEXPECTED RETURN

Ariel half expected to find the bookstore still locked up and dark when she got there, but the note in the window was gone, the iron gate across the doorway had been folded back to the sides, a little black and white sign saying OPEN hung in the oval window in the door, and she could just make out the dull glow of hanging lamps through the glass to either side. A tentative pull on the door handle found it unlocked. She pushed it open, setting a little bell chiming, and stepped inside.

Most bookstores she'd visited had walls, tables, advertising posters, signage. This one had nothing but books. That was Ariel's first impression, and it was very nearly her final impression, too, once she'd finished looking around. If there were walls, they were hidden behind wooden shelves that stretched from floor to ceiling, black with well-aged varnish and loaded nearly to the breaking point with books of every imaginable shape and size. More shelves loaded with more books thrust themselves out into the space in the middle, making anything like a clear view of the back of the store an exercise in futility. The only thing approximating a table was the sales counter close to the front door, and it, too, was stacked with books of every description. Of advertisements and signs there was no trace, barring little pieces of card taped to shelves here and there, bearing words obscure to Ariel: GNOSIS, THEURGY, SPAGYRICS, QUADRIVIUM. The laws of physics kept the ceiling free of books, leaving the space to a selection of hanging lamps and brown narrow-bladed ceiling fans turning listlessly as they waited for their winter hibernation. The floor was not so fortunate. Here and there, mostly in corners, stacks of books rose to knee height or higher.

A low rustle of movement sounded behind the sales counter, and a young man stood up from behind a heap of books and gave her an uncertain look. Of middle height but leaner than most, he had a thin face framed in brown hair and bushy eyebrows that crossed over the space above his nose without a break. Blue eyes looked over a pair of narrow reading glasses, took her measure. A dark green shirt with the sleeves rolled up, a black button-up vest, and gray woolen trousers with pleats in front gave him a vaguely antique look, though Ariel guessed he was no older than she was. "Hello," he said, in a tone that suggested he didn't know her and wasn't sure he wanted to. "Can I help you?"

"Yes, please," she said. "I have a message for Ms. Dupois."

"From?"

"Dr. Moravec."

His eyebrows twitched upwards as a unit. "I'll let her know."

He headed back into the dim recesses of the bookstore, leaving Ariel to glance at the books on the sales counter. Most of them had titles in languages she didn't know, and nearly half weren't even in scripts she recognized. Those she could read weren't much easier to interpret: what exactly was she to make, for example, of that blue clothbound volume labeled *Hamlet's Mill* or the red one next to it titled *The Most Holy Trinosophia*? At least, she reassured herself, there weren't any Bertie Scrubb books in sight.

She was still pondering that when the door behind her chimed and opened, and someone came into the store. Ariel glanced back over one shoulder. The newcomer was an old man, no taller than she was and not much heavier, wearing a worn dove-gray suit with narrow lapels. An improbably bright green bow tie perched under a round and wrinkled face that had probably been light-skinned once, before decades of sun and wind had turned it leather-brown. Disorderly white hair spilled out from under a floppy cap of gray wool tweed. His eyes, a pale gray that looked like polished steel in the bookstore's dim light, moved up and down, considering her. He smiled and nodded, she smiled back, and he went past her to the card that read SPAGYRICS and began examining the titles on the shelves nearby.

Mutter of uncertain sounds further back in the wilderness of books surrounding her finally sorted themselves out into footfalls, two sets of them. Ariel turned to face that way and put on a smile, but one look at the woman advancing toward her made her wonder if it was wasted effort. Dressed in a severe black skirt and a white blouse, her graying blonde hair tied up in a bun, her gray eyes focused tautly through little round frameless glasses, her square chin set hard and her mouth tensed harder still, she reminded Ariel of the stereotypical unfriendly schoolteacher in old children's books.

Ariel braced herself to say something polite, but she didn't have the chance. The woman spotted the old man who'd just entered, gasped audibly, turned toward him and said, "Mr. Cray! You're back!"

The old man looked up from an ancient leatherbound book and smiled. "Good day, Genevieve. Yes, I got off the boat this morning. I trust everything is well with you."

The woman recovered her poise with an effort. "Approximately."

That seemed to amuse him. "Why, I'm glad to hear that. I'll be in touch in a few days, once I have a place to stay and enough time to unpack."

"You'll be staying in town for a while, then?"

"That's my current plan."

She opened her mouth to say something else, and evidently thought better of it. Mr. Cray smiled and turned back to the book he was considering. After sending one more uncertain glance in the old man's direction, the woman turned to Ariel. "Good afternoon. I believe you have a message for me."

"If you're Ms. Dupois, yes," said Ariel. The woman nodded, and Ariel took the envelope from her shoulder bag and handed it over.

Ms. Dupois glanced at it, then at Ariel, and her expression changed slightly: not enough to suggest a smile, not even enough to remove the general look of disapproval, but a faint waning of the chill, as though the lethal cold of the Arctic winter had given way to a more ordinarily icy January night. "Ah. You must be Dr. Moravec's granddaughter. Ariel, I believe?"

"Yes," said Ariel.

Ms. Dupois reached out a hand. "Genevieve Dupois. Pleased to meet you."

If she was, she didn't show any sign of it, but Ariel pressed her hand anyway and said something polite, paused to make sure nothing else was called for, then said her goodbyes and turned to go. Before she could start for the door, though, the old man said, "Miss Moravec? If I could delay you for just a moment."

Ariel turned back to face him. "Sure."

"So you're Bernard's granddaughter." He considered her for a moment. "Perhaps you could let him know that Theophilus Cray's arrived in town. Better still—" He extracted a flat silver box from inside his coat, pulled out a business card, took a pen from a different pocket, wrote something on it and handed it to Ariel. "Is he still living on Lyon Street, next to the park? Excellent. Let him know I'd be pleased to call on him sometime soon."

"I'll tell him," Ariel said, and put the card in her shoulder bag. Another round of goodbyes, and she left the bookshop. Her last glimpse inside the shop before the door closed was of the young man who'd first greeted her. He was watching her go with a look on his face that was a little puzzled and a little wary, but seemed to hide something else behind those that she couldn't read at all.

Outside traffic growled and muttered. A sharp autumn wind had risen, bringing the scents of fallen leaves and woodsmoke through the stench of tailpipe fumes. Ariel got her bearings and set out through the tag-ends of Adocentyn's downtown into the neighborhood of old ornate mansions and little green parks that surrounded the Heydonian. The maps she'd studied in the library came to mind as she walked, reminding her that a few centuries before, the ground she walked on had been fields of corn and pastures for cows and pigs, with a few farmhouses scattered among them and ancient oak forest still spilling nearly halfway down Culpeper Hill. She passed the Heydonian Institution itself, serene behind its fluted pillars and soaring many-windowed marble walls, and kept going.

Most of a dozen blocks later, Oak Avenue drew a line across her journey, and as she crossed it she reminded herself that she was on the Curdie estate, where the old pirate had spent the latter part of his life. Somewhere in that section of the Culpeper Hill neighborhood, he'd built a house, and if the treasure existed at all it might be there, or somewhere close by—but where? The comfortable Victorian homes she passed had nothing to say on the subject. How many other people, she wondered, had walked down those same streets, asking themselves the same question, and gotten no answer?

Her grandfather's house loomed up in front of her presently, and she pushed aside thoughts about the treasure long enough to let herself in. The ground floor was utterly silent, and a note on the kitchen table explained why: *Ariel—I'll be at the Heydonian until late. Pizza?* That last word brought pleasant thoughts to mind, but a glance at the clock showed that she had a couple of hours at least to kill. She picked up Lévi's book, but the thought of wrestling with another chapter of his evasive French prose didn't appeal much.

She paged further back in the book, found herself looking at a diagram of a five-pointed star surrounded by baffling letters and symbols, and then flipped nearly all the way to the back. That landed her at a list headed *Spirits of the Sixth Hour* with odd names below it: Tabris, Susabo, Eirnilus, Nitira, Haatan, Hatiphas, and Zaren, each with some special function. Those interested her, but a glance back at the share of the book in her left hand showed more than 300 pages to go before she got there. She let out an exasperated sigh and shut the book. Lacking anything better to do, she went up to her room to put her shoulder bag away and find a temporary home for the two books on Captain Curdie.

It was when she turned toward her desk and half noticed the two clippings she'd left there that the memory she'd chased at the library finally surfaced. She stopped, let the shoulder bag drop down all anyhow on the floor, and read through both clippings. Then, just to be certain, she sat at the desk, found a piece of paper, made a little sketch map of the Culpeper Hill neighborhood, and marked down both the places the clipping mentioned, and then the two other sightings she'd heard mentioned at Aunt Clarice's a few days before.

She'd known in an instant what the map would show, but seeing it in ink on paper made the insight even more definite. All four of the places where the masked daylight prowler had been seen were within the boundaries of the old Curdie estate. She went over the map again, in case she could spot any pattern in the sightings, without result. Once again, a dim whisper of memory stirred, but she wasn't able to coax it to the surface and turned her attention to the few scraps of information she had.

Was the prowler looking for the treasure? That was the first thought that occurred to Ariel, but it didn't explain the mask or the secretive, skulking way he made his rounds. If he was doing nothing more nefarious than looking for signs of Captain Curdie's house, why didn't he just stroll through the neighborhood, or get a dog and take it for walks down the streets he wanted to explore? It would attract much less attention. She put the question aside for later.

A few minutes later she curled up on the sofa downstairs with a cup of tea and the book by Delphinia Braddock she'd gotten from the library. It turned out to be a lively piece of 1970s journalism, more concerned with the antics of the people who'd gone searching for the treasure down through the years than with the pirate captain or the treasure itself. It had a photo section halfway through, a dozen glossy pages with black and white pictures. The first of them caught her attention instantly: an eighteenth-century portrait of a middle-aged man in an ornate periwig, the sort of wig that rich men wore in colonial times. Heavy brows, a hooked nose, and loose jowls: that was her first impression. She glanced down at the caption, found that she was looking at a portrait of Captain Bartholomew Curdie. She considered him for a time, and then turned to the beginning of the first chapter and started reading.

The book itself was sufficiently well written that she was still in the midst of it when the front door rattled and Dr. Moravec came in. She knew his ways well enough by then that when she spotted the preoccupied look on his face, she didn't waste time on a greeting he wouldn't hear. Instead, she waited until he was in his study, went to the kitchen, made a second cup of tea, and settled back on the sofa to finish her book. She hadn't quite finished the last chapter when he came back out of the study and noticed her existence. "Good afternoon. I hope my dinner suggestion was welcome."

"If I ever don't say yes to pizza, make sure I have a pulse."

She couldn't be entirely sure from his expression, or lack of one, whether he realized that she was joking. They settled the toppings promptly anyway, and Dr. Moravec went into the kitchen to phone in the order. Once that was done and various sounds told of another cup of tea being prepared, he came back out and settled into his armchair.

"I gave your message to Ms. Dupois," Ariel said then.

"Thank you."

"But I also have a couple of messages for you. The book-shop was closed when I got there and I ended up going into St. Cyprian's Church to waste some time and look for Captain Curdie's gravestone. Is Margaret Hynd the minister there?"

Both his eyebrows rose noticeably. "Yes, she is."

"She said I should give you her best regards."

"Did she indeed." His face did not shift at all.

"She said you'd be surprised, because the two of you dis-agreed about some things."

That earned her, to her surprise, a little dry laugh. "That's an understatement, but I won't argue the point. She's on the Heydonian's Board of Trustees—did she mention that? Good. There are various opinions about how the Institution should adapt to changing times, and her opinion and mine differ more than most. Doubtless it's healthy for the organization, but we've had harsh things to say to each other from time to time." He paused, considered her. "Did you mention to her that you were going to speak with Genevieve Dupois?"

"Nope. We talked about Captain Curdie and the treasure, and she said I should go to the downtown library. I did, too."

Dr. Moravec nodded. "Good. And the other message?"

"A funny little man came into Ms. Dupois's bookshop when I was there. After Ms. Dupois mentioned your name he gave me this—" She'd brought the business card downstairs with her and used it as a bookmark in Delphinia Braddock's book; it took her one moment to find it and another to get up and hand it to Dr. Moravec.

The old man took it and blinked in surprise. Dead silence followed as Ariel watched him, fascinated. A moment later a hint of a smile bent one side of his mouth. "Theophilus Cray," he said. "Well. That's a name I wasn't at all sure I'd ever hear again. So he's still alive, and back after all this time."

"Ms. Dupois was really surprised to see him," Ariel said. "He told her he got off the boat this morning and he's going to be staying in town for a while. He asked me if you were still living here and said he wanted to come by sometime soon."

"I'm very glad to hear that." He glanced at the card again, nodded as though to himself, and slipped it into a pocket inside his coat.

Ariel considered her grandfather for a moment, then ventured, "So who is he?"

"Theophilus Cray? That would be a very long story." He sipped tea, and for a moment Ariel thought that was all she was going to get from him. He set the cup down on the end table, though, and went on. "The shortest possible version is that he's an old friend of mine, one of the first people I met when I moved to Adocentyn. More to the point, I studied with him. We're much the same age, but he had a considerable head start. He comes from one of the oldest and richest Adocentyn families, and his grandmother was Florinda Cray, who was on the board of trustees of the Heydonian for more than half a century and wrote several very influential books on magic. Theophilus lived with her for the last ten years or so of her life, and learned a great deal from her. After she died he was very active in certain circles here. Then—" He gestured, as though scattering something to the winds. "A good many years ago now, he left Adocentyn hoping to find—certain things. There were serious dangers involved. So we said our farewells and he boarded a freighter and sailed away."

Ariel blinked. "I didn't know you could even do that any more."

"Yes, quite a few freighters still have a few cabins they rent out to passengers. I've traveled that way myself. It's slower than air travel but it has its charms."

"Certain things," Ariel said then. "Did he tell anyone what those were?"

"Of course. When he visits, I'll let him tell that part of the story if he chooses."

Ariel stifled her disappointment and nodded. A change of subject came to mind. "I went to the fourth floor of the downtown library. They've got all the old books up there, and a card catalog. Any idea why?"

"Yes, as it happens. One of our little local controversies." He sipped more tea. "Eighteen years ago, I think it was, the library system hired a new head librarian from some other state. The first thing she tried to do once she arrived was to get rid of every book in the library's collection that was more than ten years old."

Ariel gave him a horrified look, and he shrugged. "A common bad habit in some circles. Adocentyn being Adocentyn, there was a public outcry, and she backed down, more or less. Instead of discarding the books, she had them all moved to the fourth floor and left out of the library's online catalog, hoping that people would forget about them. That simply made her critics go out of their way to check out those books. She lasted five years and then went to some West Coast city or other, but the books stayed on the fourth floor and nobody's managed to find the funding to get them into the online catalog. So there they are, and you have to go to the downtown library to find out what's in that part of the collection."

"There was an old book on Captain Curdie," said Ariel, and held up the volume.

"Good," he said. "In the meantime, have you made any more progress with Lévi?"

She reddened. "No. He's my after dinner reading today."

Dr. Moravec nodded, said nothing. Ariel tried to keep the blush from deepening, and failed dismally. Finally she said, "Maybe I don't know as much French as I thought. I keep on reading him and then wondering if I've understood a single word."

He shook his head. "The problem isn't the language. The problem is that Lévi expects you to think like a mage."

The words Ariel wanted to say were "But what if I can't?" but she knew instantly what response that would get her. Instead, she nodded glumly, and tried to convince herself that she wasn't as lost as she felt.

CHAPTER 7

A RULE OF THREE

The next morning, Saturday morning, Ariel blinked awake earlier than usual with a sudden insistent memory at the forefront of her mind. Through the window nearest her bed, morning sun glittered on the windows of Adocentyn's Art Deco-era skyscrapers, and clouds piled up behind them, gilded with light; she scarcely noticed. Once she'd showered, dressed, and ruffled the fur on Nicodemus's head, she went downstairs and headed straight for the kitchen.

The old house was as quiet as it ever got, with only a faint mutter of distant traffic for soundtrack. Her grandfather wasn't up yet. She took a few moments to get coffee started and bread in the toaster, and then hefted the stack of newspapers from its place beside the recycle bin and started going back over the last three weeks of police blotter columns, looking for something she knew she'd find.

By the time she'd finished the hunt, she'd made and eaten the toast and was on her second mug of coffee, but she had a little stack of clippings on the table. The papers went back to their place, and she took the clippings upstairs to put next to the two she'd gotten earlier. A glance over the sketch map she'd drawn erased her last doubts. The masked prowler had been spotted and reported to the police half a dozen times before the clipping that first caught her attention, and every one of the reports had placed him in the part of the Culpeper Hill neighborhood that had once been owned by Captain Curdie.

She brooded over that as she went back downstairs and got the Saturday paper, which was sitting as usual on the front step. Turning the pages to the day's police blotter got her heart ever so slightly aflutter, but it was all for nothing: there was no shortage of things to clip for her grandfather's files, but the prowler hadn't put in another appearance. She was still frowning about that when the phone rang, and she got up and answered it without remembering that it was Saturday morning.

That was a mistake. She knew that, and flinched, as soon as she heard the voice on the other end of the line. "Ariel? I want to know what you're doing about your future," the voice said. It was her mother, of course. Ariel had put an end to a daily bombardment of texts from that source by the simple expedient of snapping her smartphone in half and dropping it into Coopers Bay one lovely summer morning, shortly after she'd arranged to stay in Adocentyn for good. The kitchen phone couldn't be discarded so easily, though Ariel had thought about it more than once on Saturday mornings. That was always when her mother called.

She said something bland in response to the question, and braced herself for a lecture. Nor was she disappointed. For the next twenty minutes or so her mother told her in lavish detail just how big a mistake it was for her to waste her life in a low-paying job when she still had the chance to claw her way into a salaried position and a corporate career. It wasn't the first time Ariel had heard that lecture, or for that matter the hundred and first; she knew better than to try to explain yet again to her mother that she'd rather tear out her eyes than spend her days in a cubicle farm, or that she was happier in Adocentyn than she'd been since childhood; instead, she bit her tongue, made a mental checklist of the usual points of her mother's lecture, marked them off one at a time as they came up, and tried to keep her temper.

By the time the lecture wound up, despite all her efforts, Ariel was fuming inwardly. When her mother finally drew breath and said, "Well? Don't you have anything to say?" she paused just long enough to let the silence get uncomfortable. Then, as calmly as she could: "You left out the part about how much I'm going to regret it when I'm old and poor and living in a little apartment without even a cat to keep me company. Or was it a dog? I forget."

That got the sudden angry silence she'd hoped for. A moment passed. "I'm just worried about you," the voice said, in a brittle tone. "You need to face facts."

Those last words turned out to be just that little bit too much for Ariel's self-control. "We went through this six years ago," she snapped. "And you know what? I haven't changed my mind. I'm not going to change my mind. I'm happy where I am, I've got a job and a place to live, I know you think I ought to want your kind of life but I don't. Okay? So maybe you ought to face a fact or two yourself one of these days."

Words like those usually earned her either dead silence or a diatribe. This time she got the dead silence, and then a few words in an even more brittle tone. "I'll call again when you've had time to calm down and be reasonable. Good-bye." A click punctuated the last word, leaving dead air and then, after another moment, a dial tone.

Ariel didn't throw the handset against the wall, but it was a close thing. Instead she made herself hang up the handset as gently as she could—her hands were shaking, but she managed it anyway—and turned away sharply toward the kitchen window.

"I wish," she said in a low hard voice, "that she would just ... shut ... *up*." The words hung in the quiet air, mocking her, and it didn't help that she knew better than to think that it would happen. It didn't help, either, that she knew that her mother really was worried about her, and simply couldn't understand that Ariel didn't want the same kind of life she'd chosen.

Minutes passed. Ariel walked over to the window and stared moodily through it at the rose garden behind the house. Off past the roses, the fence, and the house behind, Culpeper Hill sloped raggedly eastward toward Lambspring Point. Sun and cloud chased each other across the sky. She was still looking out the window, trying to make herself think about Captain Curdie and colonial Adocentyn and not getting far, when the phone rang again.

She turned and glared at it, then remembered that her mother never called back immediately after one of their fights. It still took her an effort to go over to the phone and pick up the handset. The voice that answered her, though, wasn't one she knew at all: a man's voice, somewhere in the tenor range. "Hello," it said, with more than a hint of uncertainty. "May I speak to Dr. Moravec?"

Ariel put on her best professional voice. "I'm sorry, he's not available right now. Can I take a message?"

She could indeed. The caller gave his name, Clarence Harshaw, and his number, and those went onto the notepad beside the phone. A click on the line, and Ariel hung up the phone, feeling a little less morose. She got herself another cup of coffee, then went to work on the morning paper, clipping out the stories her grandfather wanted to see.

There was only one story about the Heydonian Institution that day, and nothing at all that answered to most of the categories on her grandfather's list, but the bottom of the local section's first page had something that more than made up for that. PRICELESS ANTIQUE GOES MISSING, the headline yelled, and the columns of text below it filled in the details: the most expensive item in the Denby-Adams collection of antiques had vanished in the last week. There were no witnesses and no suspects. Someone had slipped into one of the big mansions not far from the Heydonian sometime in the previous week and made off with a topaz shewstone in a gilt silver frame, an item which had belonged to Elias Ashmole himself.

Ariel wondered what a shewstone might be, but set the question aside for the moment. The scissors did their job, and she added the paragraphs on the front page and the half page further back that rounded out the story to the stack of clippings.

She'd begun one final pass through the Saturday paper when the phone rang again. Ariel tensed, knowing that it might possibly be her mother this time, but decided to pick up the call anyway. To her relief, it was another unfamiliar voice, an elderly woman, asking the same thing as Clarence Harshaw. Another name and phone number went onto the note she'd made earlier.

The clippings and the note with the names and phone numbers went onto the end table next to the armchair her grandfather favored. She'd just left them there and started back toward the kitchen to refill her coffee mug when the phone rang again. Ariel braced herself, but once again it was an unfamiliar voice, an old man with a hint of a French accent. The same question got the same answer. Ariel took another message and went back into the parlor with her coffee, shaking her head.

The older book on Captain Curdie's treasure waited for her, but the fight with her mother had put her in a mulish mood and she picked up Lévi's book instead and flung herself into it. She'd reached the start of the third chapter—*Le verbe parfait, c'est ternaire*, it began, and she translated the whole sentence without much effort: *Perfect speech is threefold, because it assumes a principle that understands, a principle that speaks, and a principle that is spoken.*

Okay, she thought. So? The page didn't favor her with an answer, and when she went further she quickly found herself in a tangle of prose in which philosophy, theology, and magic seemed all muddled up together. She gritted her teeth and kept reading. The chapter was only six pages long, which helped, and she made herself go all the way to the end. She was a few sentences from the end when a whisper of footsteps from the stair told her that her grandfather was on his way down.

She finished just before he rounded the foot of the stair and came into sight, but a certain brittle pride kept her from putting the book away before he'd seen it. His glance, indecipherable as always, passed over her, and he nodded a silent greeting and went into the kitchen. He had his invariable routine first thing in the mornings, and she'd already learned to track its stages by the sounds he made: splash of water into a battered sauce-pan, clank of the saucepan on the stove, sigh of the refrigerator door opening and shutting, and then a long pause before the water boiled and a little flurry of sounds as eggs got poached, toast made, kippers extracted from their can, and coffee filled a cup already prepared with cream and sugar. The whole pro-cess took him a little over seven minutes without fail. Ariel put the time into glancing back over the chapter of Lévi's book, then blushed as she thought about what he'd think of her try-ing to show off, and hurriedly put the book back on the end table just before he came out.

"Good morning," he said as he emerged from the kitchen, plate in one hand and coffee mug in the other. "I believe I heard more than one phone call."

"Yeah. One from my mother."

"My condolences."

That forced out a little choked laugh. "Thanks. The other three were for you. You're popular this morning."

He settled in his armchair and got his breakfast and coffee settled, then picked up the stack of clippings and the two notes and went through them while sipping coffee and eating one of the kippers. "Ah," he said partway through the process. Ariel waited, and finally he went on. "I'll be interested to see which of the callers want to talk about Theophilus Cray and which of them want to talk about the Denby-Adams shews-tone." He pronounced the last word as though it was spelled "showstone."

Ariel waited a moment, and then said, "Is it okay if I ask a question?" He gestured, inviting it, and she went on. "What's a shewstone?"

"An instrument for scrying." When Ariel's face betrayed her uncertainty: "Scrying's what some people nowadays call remote viewing, or clairvoyance: seeing things beyond the range of normal vision. You've seen the crystal balls Clarice has in her shop, I believe? Those are shewstones, of one popular type."

"Yeah. Okay, that makes sense. And this one was Elias Ashmole's?"

"Exactly. He brought it here with him when he founded Adocentyn, and it was ancient even in his time, older than anything else he brought with him. It's a rare item, and worth a great deal of money, but of course it also has magical uses. Quite a few people will be concerned about what might be done with it."

She nodded, and ventured: "But Mr. Cray's just as important."

"Good." Dr. Moravec sipped more coffee. "Very good. Yes, in a certain sense."

Ariel had already gotten used to the hard fact that sometimes, "in a certain sense" was one of the ways her grandfather said "and I don't intend to say any more about the subject just now." She downed some of her own coffee to hide her disappointment, and reached for the end table next to her, meaning to pick up the book on Captain Curdie's treasure. She blinked in surprise to find Eliphas Lévi's book in her hand instead, then remembered that she'd put it down without looking a few moments before. The book reminded her of earlier perplexities, and she decided to see if there was a way around those. "Can I ask another question?"

"Of course."

"I read chapter three of the first half today." She raised the book to make sure he knew what she was talking about, and he nodded. "All about threes. I'm pretty sure I don't have a clue what he's talking about."

"Quite the contrary," he replied, unruffled. "You simply don't realize it yet." He paused, and for a moment she was sure he meant to drop the subject, but he went on: "Human beings habitually think in twos—this or that, yes or no, good or bad, and so on. The world's not as simple as that, and a good many of the mistakes that make our lives miserable are because we can't see that there are more than two options. That's one of the things that Lévi's talking about. I'll hazard a guess: your mother this morning only talked about two possibilities."

"Yeah," Ariel said after a moment. "Yeah, she did. Either I get a corporate job like hers or I spend my whole life flipping burgers and starving in an attic."

"Exactly. And what's the third option?"

"Living here and working for you," said Ariel. Then: "But there are other things I could have done instead."

"Good!" He gestured at her with his fork, ornamented just then with half a kippered fish. "That's one of the secrets of the ternary. Once you break out of a binary and see a third option, it's quite likely you can see a fourth, a fifth, and so on. Do you recall what Lévi wrote about the pillars of the temple of Solomon?" When she nodded: "The doorway was between the pillars. Identify the two ends of the binary and look between them, and there's your doorway."

She nodded again, more slowly.

"But there's more to the rule of three than that. Think of what Lévi wrote about *le verbe parfait*. It has three parts: the speaker, the listener, and the word itself. That's true of everything: there's an active side, a receptive side and the act itself. If you can see all three aspects, well and good. If you can only see two, you know that there must be a third, and you can triangulate from what you know to what you don't know. Think of the business in Criswell this summer. We knew who was on the receiving end of the witchcraft, and what kind of witchcraft was being done."

"Well, you did," said Ariel.

"You worked it out soon enough. But it was simply a matter of taking those two facts as starting points and looking for clues that would identify the third point of the triangle."

"Okay," she said after a moment. "Yeah, I can see that." She opened the book again, and Dr. Moravec turned his attention to his remaining poached egg.

Just then the phone in the kitchen rang again. Reflexes she'd spent six weeks cultivating took over; she plopped the book down on the sofa and launched herself toward the kitchen before it occurred to her that it might be her mother calling back. No help for it, she decided, and picked up the phone anyway.

"Good morning," said an elderly woman whose voice Ariel was sure she'd never heard before. "Perhaps I could speak to Dr. Moravec?"

"Just a moment," Ariel said, suppressing a sigh of relief. She set the phone down and stuck her head through the doorway into the parlor. "It's for you."

Her grandfather nodded, set his coffee mug down, and extracted himself from the armchair. Ariel went back to the sofa and retrieved the book, aware of his deep voice in the kitchen but trying, without too much success, not to snoop.

A speaker, a listener, and a word, she thought. The prowler's saying something, whether he knows it or not, and sneaking around the neighborhood in daylight with a mask on his face is how he's saying it.

Who's listening?

CHAPTER 8

A GLINT OF BRIGHTNESS

By the time she'd washed up the morning dishes two more people had called for Dr. Moravec, and he'd told her in his diffident way that he'd need the parlor and privacy for several hours shortly. A glance out the windows showed sunlight and blue sky chasing away the last of the morning's clouds. That, a certain restlessness, and a memory from a few days before sent her upstairs to her room to fetch her purse; she stopped just long enough to stuff her sketch map into it and ruffle Nicodemus's fur. When she got back downstairs her grandfather glanced up from his chair and said, "A pleasant day for a walk."

She nodded. "And a little shopping."

That got her a look with one eyebrow raised. In response, she started singing, to a tune familiar to every American child:

> "There's a place in France
> Where the ladies have no pants,
> But I don't live there,
> So I need some things to wear."

Dr. Moravec made a little choked noise somewhere down in his throat, which might have been a laugh's second cousin. One hand waved her toward the front door. She grinned and took the hint.

Outside sunlight streamed down from a blue autumn sky onto Lyon Avenue and the old houses that lined it, and leaves of half a dozen colors tossed and fluttered in the wind. Ariel walked the block and a half downhill to Ivy Street and turned left, toward Lambspring Point. The shops on Ivy, upscale for the first two blocks, slid from there as the street bent down the eastern side of Culpeper Hill, shedding brand-name coffee places and glossy-looking boutiques and filling in the gaps with dry cleaners, storefront churches, and dollar stores.

A few more blocks, and an ungainly former warehouse loomed up on the far side of a much-patched parking lot half full of slightly battered cars. The sign on the building spelled out words she'd heard from Teresa Kozlowski a few days before, and the sight of it sent her heart very slightly aflutter.

For the last few years of her life, in point of fact, she had gone out of her way to cultivate a vice. It was admittedly not one of the vices discussed by street preachers or the tabloids she saw in grocery checkout lines. Drugs didn't interest her, and neither did gambling; the one time she'd gotten drunk, back in her sophomore year of high school, the experience had been miserable enough that she'd never wanted to repeat it; the few parties she'd attended mostly consisted of having to fend off passes from boys she didn't like, and while the thought of getting very close someday to a boy she did like was far from displeasing to her, the opportunity hadn't yet presented itself. The simple fact that none of those habits would have upset her mother unduly took more than half the attraction away from them, and guided her instead straight across the parking lot to the slightly dilapidated double doors of the Ivy Street Thrift Emporium and her private obsession: cheap secondhand antique clothes.

Inside the Emporium, fluorescent fixtures that had seen half a century of hard use poured out a bleak grayish light on a big echoing space full of shelves, clothing racks, and a motley but genial collection of shoppers. Ariel found a cart, took a few moments to find her bearings, and then made a beeline to the women's clothing section. A little further searching got her past the long parade of ordinary dresses, blouses, and pants to more interesting things. Finer fabrics and better workmanship than anyone produced any more, and the styles of a more elegant era: those were the things that mattered, or so she told herself. In the back of her mind, though, was the thought of her mother's shocked and scornful response—"You're wearing someone else's *clothes?*"—and that was what made secondhand clothes irresistible.

Not all of them deserved that last adjective, to be sure. Ariel glanced over two fussy satin gowns that somebody's great-grandmother must have worn to formal dinners in the 1950s, turned up her nose at a rose taffeta aberration that some unusually callous bride must have inflicted on her bridesmaids, marveled at the dubious taste of a gown with long sleeves and knife-pleat skirt in an improbable shade of teal polyester, and considered and regretfully decided against a golden silk cheongsam cut for a woman a good six inches taller and wider than she was. The next item on the rack, though, set her pulse racing.

It was a classic little black dress of wool crepe with cap sleeves, the sort of thing she imagined New York socialites wearing at cocktail parties in the middle of the previous century. She pulled it out, glanced at the tag inside the neckline and a little gasp burst from her when she found that it would fit. A close examination inside and out revealed no stains, no holes, no seams about to give way. Holding her breath, she checked the price tag, and whispered a little thank you to nobody in particular: the dress was well within her budget. Quickly, in case some unseen rival was waiting to pounce on it, she put the dress in her shopping cart and went on.

The rest of the rack offered nothing to tempt her. With her immediate cravings sated, she looked around again, and spotted a familiar face a few aisles away: Teresa Kozlowski, maneuvering a shopping cart already well stocked with what looked like children's clothes. Ariel grinned and waved, and Teresa caught the motion, smiled, and waved back.

Off the other direction was the store's book section, a collection of battered and mismatched bookshelves along one wall. That looked promising, and she went that way, but what first met her glance were two entire shelves full of Bertie Scrubb novels. She gave the brightly colored volumes an irritable look, then consoled herself with the thought that so many readers found the popular series disappointing enough to donate their copies to a thrift store.

She went on, glanced at two volumes that looked old enough to be interesting: a collection of Dashiell Hammett short stories and a novel she hadn't read yet by Somerset Maugham, a new favorite author of hers. They each cost fifty cents and so both of them went into her cart. A little later she spotted a battered textbook with the words GREGG SHORTHAND on the spine. That intrigued her. She pulled it from the shelf, opened it, and considered the quaint ink-and-wash drawings of office staff at work and the pages of weird little scribbles that meant whole words. Aunt Clarice's passing comment stirred in her mind, and so did details from the 1920s fiction she loved: wasn't shorthand what secretaries used back then? She glanced at a few more pages, checked the price, and put the book in her cart with the others.

Beyond the book section was another random assortment of shelves, heaped with an even more random assortment of items for sale. She went along the shelves as much from curiosity as anything else, the way she'd walked along the beach on summer vacations in childhood to see what the waves had brought up that day. Most of what cluttered the shelves might as well have been half-dried seaweed, and two Bertie Scrubb action figures made her curl her lip as though she'd found an unusually ripe fish, but one glittering shell caught her eye: a pleasant little painted resin statue of a wolf, its muzzle raised to howl. She didn't need it, she told herself, but it cost less than a dollar, and a childhood full of small treasures capriciously taken away—"You don't need that any more," her mother would say, and make off with some anchor for hopes and dreams Ariel hadn't hidden carefully enough—made her suddenly stubborn. The wolf went into her shopping cart next to the books.

The other item that interested her was an old film camera, a Kodak Brownie from sometime well back in the previous century. It cost more than she wanted to pay, and she realized that she had no way to tell if it was in working order or not, but its presence there stirred a memory: the day she'd snapped her smartphone in half and sent the pieces to the bottom of Coopers Bay, she'd decided to look into film cameras. She made a mental note, then thought better of that, got a pen and a spiral bound notepad out of her purse, and wrote a note to herself.

None of the other sections of the Emporium seemed to offer anything of interest, so Ariel headed toward the checkstands at the front of the store. Only one of them had a cashier just then. Ariel got in line behind an elderly black woman whose cart had two carefully chosen dresses and a big presentation Bible in it. Moments later, Teresa Kozlowski joined the line. Her cart was full: on top of the clothes she'd had earlier rose a great heap of bright-colored skeins of yarn.

"Fancy meeting you here," Ariel said.

That earned her a laugh. "I could say the same thing."

Ariel made a little shrug. "I live pretty close. This place is just as good as you said, too." She motioned at the cart between them. "But it looks like you hit the jackpot."

Teresa's face brightened. "Oh, yes. The place Lucy and I went Thursday had plenty of things in Joey's size but almost nothing in Lucy's, and she's growing like a weed these days. Today was my next day off, so I came here. I found some clothes that'll fit her, and then—well, there's a women's group at my church that knits hats, scarves, baby blankets, things like that to give to poor people. I'm part of that when I have the time, but I also keep an eye open for yarn, because some of the ladies don't have any money to spare but they love to knit. So when I saw all this yarn, and so cheap, I knew the Lord meant me to get it for them. Now I just have to figure out how to get everything back home—I walked here."

"It's just three blocks to your place, right? I can help carry it if you want."

"Would you? That would be so kind of you."

"Easy. All I have is a dress, a little statue and a few books," said Ariel.

Once they'd both paid up, Ariel hefted her own bag and two big plastic bags of yarn and followed Teresa out the door and into the parking lot. "That's really nice," said Ariel, "that you and the other church ladies do that. Make scarves and things, I mean."

"I really wish I could do more. I don't know if you're a religious person, but—" Teresa managed a slight shrug, though it took an effort not to spill yarn. "So many people have so much less than I do. I hate to think that somebody might get sick just because I didn't do something kind for them."

Ariel thought about that as they got to Holly Avenue and waited for the light to turn. "If I see some cheap yarn someplace, should I pick it up for you?"

"Would you please? Only please make sure that it's acrylic. A lot of poor people don't have the time to hand wash wool and they don't have a good place to air dry it, and of course if you launder it, it's ruined. One time we had somebody donate a lot of fancy alpaca yarn, and we couldn't use it at all. But Ruth Kolchak knew somebody who wanted it and would trade us acrylic yarn for it. So it worked out that time."

"Acrylic," Ariel said. "Got it." A memory stirred: a little storefront not far from the Culpeper Hill branch of the public library, where she went often. "There's a yarn store by the library on Cedar Street, isn't there?"

"I don't know," Teresa admitted. "Paul ought to know, though. He goes to the library there sometimes when he feels well enough, and brings home all kinds of books. I'm not much of a reader—well, other than the Bible and my missal and my St. Joseph prayer book. Just one of those things, I suppose."

Cars went rushing by on Holly Avenue, and a sudden rush of wind off Coopers Bay joined them. That made the bags of yarn difficult to maneuver for a block or two, and Ariel had to concentrate on keeping any of the skeins from spilling onto the sidewalk. By the time the wind calmed again, the stair to the Kozlowski house was close by.

They managed to get their respective burdens up the stairs and in the front door without losing anything. The parlor offered calmer weather; it was as shabby and cluttered as before, and a little boy—Joey, Ariel guessed—was sitting in one corner, preoccupied with a stuffed bear with bright blue fur. Once the bags of yarn and clothing landed next to the sofa, Teresa said, "Can I get you some coffee or something? That was really very sweet of you to help." Ariel made the appropriate noises, and Teresa started for the kitchen.

Before she could get there, Lucy came trotting down the hall. "Mom? Uncle Paul says something's wrong in the bathroom."

Teresa flinched visibly. "Okay," she said, putting on a smile she obviously didn't feel. "Thank you, Lucy." To Ariel: "Sorry. I hope this'll just be a minute."

She vanished into the back part of the house, and Lucy came over to Ariel. "Hi." She turned to her brother. "Joey? This is the detective I told you about. She's nice."

Ariel let herself be led over to the child and his stuffed bear. The bear was sitting up in front of him, facing him, and something small and bright sat on the floor between them. After they'd been introduced by Lucy, Ariel said, "So are you going to introduce me to your bear?"

The child beamed. "Sure. His name's Albert. Albert Bear."

"Pleased to meet you, Albert," said Ariel. The bright thing between child and bear was a clear plastic disk, maybe the lens from an old flashlight. "So what are you and Albert doing?"

The smile on Joey's face went away, and he hunched down. "'m not supposed to tell," he said. "I promised."

"Well, then, let's pretend I didn't ask," Ariel said at once.

Before she could say anything else, Teresa's voice came down the hall, agonized: "Oh, *no*." Ariel and the children both looked that way reflexively. A moment passed, and another, and then Teresa came back into the parlor.

"I'm terribly sorry," she said, "but one of the pipes inside the wall's broken or something, and there's water damage all through the plaster. I'm going to have to empty out the linen closet and see what else is wrong. We'll have to have that coffee another day."

Paul came into the room just then, leaning on his cane. "Oh, hello. Ms. Moravec, wasn't it? Good to see you again. I hope you're having a better day than we are."

"She helped me haul all this yarn back from the thrift store," said Teresa. "And now—" She struggled to hold back tears. "I don't know what we're going to do."

"What you're going to do," said Paul, "is call Phil Benedetti. You remember him, the guy who did all that work for the Wozniaks and let them pay when they could?"

"Yes, I remember him," said Teresa. "But I don't know—"

"Don't be silly," Paul said. "You've helped so many people, you need to let somebody help you for a change."

Teresa nodded, looking flustered, and said nothing. Ariel waited for a moment and then said, "Of course I can come back some other day. Here." She dug her notepad out of her purse, wrote her name and phone number on a blank sheet, tore it out and handed it to Teresa. "Give me a call when you've got a little time."

"Thank you," Teresa said. Turning to Paul: "You're probably right. I'll give Mr. Benedetti a call."

A minute or so later, after saying her goodbyes, Ariel went down the stairs onto Holly Avenue and looked around. The day was bright if blustery, and she still had some time to kill. As soon as she'd decided to go out that morning, she'd thought about wandering through the neighborhood and going past each of the places where the masked prowler had been spotted: the opportunity awaited. A glance at the sketch map got her headed toward the nearest spot.

A working class neighborhood for sure, Ariel thought as she set a casual pace along Penn Street. The houses there, most of them colonial or not much more recent, had almost all been divided up into flats or apartments, with doorbells and mailboxes clustered beside the entries and a general air of quiet desolation. Few cars moved along the street and fewer still were parked by the curbs; though it was Saturday, most of the people who lived there were at work or running errands. The thought of a daylight prowler going mostly unnoticed made more sense to her.

The corner of Penn and Hazel, the first place the prowler had been seen, could have passed for any other street corner in the neighborhood. An old woman's face peering out a third floor window at Ariel suggested where the newspaper had gotten its information. Ariel glanced up, sent a smile up at the face, and wondered if she'd appear on the blotter page in a day or so. From there she went up Hazel Avenue and found her way to the second spot on the sketch map, and then to the third, a block away. If anything set those two spots apart from the rest of Adocentyn's old residential neighborhoods, Ariel couldn't see it.

She went downhill a block to Gold Street, then, and spotted something she recognized, a name on a painted wooden sign:

PHIL BENEDETTI, CONTRACTOR
LICENSED AND BONDED #350880
NO JOB TOO SMALL

It was on the wall of a pleasant-looking gray house three stories tall with the usual clapboard siding, and some Victorian woodwork here and there. It had a big double garage next to it, and signs on both garage doors saying SMILE—YOU'RE ON CAMERA. The cameras themselves were up under the eaves of the house where casual vandals couldn't get to them. If Benedetti did his own home repairs, Ariel thought, the Kozlowskis could do much worse; the house was in better shape than most of the buildings she'd seen that day.

She walked on past, and spotted someone walking toward her on the sidewalk ahead. The figure in the black coat was familiar, but more than a minute passed before she got close enough to realize that she'd met the man before. All his attention was fixed on the houses he passed; he seemed oblivious to her until they were a few yards apart, then faced her with a sudden start and a look of surprise.

"Why, Ms. Moravec," said Father Vincent Novak. "A pleasant day for a walk."

"Hi," Ariel said. "Yeah, it is." Then, with a grin: "I didn't know priests got to do that."

Father Novak laughed. It was a tired laugh, and thin. "In a manner of speaking. I've just paid a visit to one member of my congregation who's feeling ill, and I'll be stopping in to see another in a few minutes."

"I hope they both feel better," Ariel said. The words sounded empty even as she said them, but she couldn't think of anything else to add.

"So do I." He shook his head. "So do I. God bless you, Ms. Moravec."

"Thanks," said Ariel, feeling even more at a loss for words. The priest smiled and went on. Ariel started walking. When she got to the corner she glanced back the way she'd come, and saw Father Novak standing only a short distance from where he'd been, watching her. As he saw her looking toward him, he turned and hurried away.

CHAPTER 9

A RUMOR OF TREASURE

"Oh, it runs in the family," said Cassie. Monday had arrived, and she and Ariel were in the back room of Aunt Clarice's shop again, garbling herbs: angelica, this time. It had a sweet aromatic scent Ariel decided she liked.

"Star names?"

Cassie waggled a finger at her. "Nope. Constellation names. Groups of stars."

Ariel nodded, kept her focus on the seeds she was extracting from a tangled brown mass of dried plant. Behind her, rain hammered on the windows, turned the alley behind the shop into a vague gray blur. A sharp peal of thunder drowned out the rain-sounds briefly, faded into distant irritable grumblings.

"My younger brothers are Orion and Eridanus," Cassie went on. "Danny's what everyone calls him, of course. My older sister's Andromeda. Dad's Leo, grandpa's Perseus, and my great-grandpa, who I never met, was Cepheus. His dad was the one that started it all, Professor Marcus Jackson. He started out as a sharecropper's kid and ended up with a Ph.D, teaching science at a college in Tennessee. He adored astronomy, he had a big telescope he'd take out on dark nights with his students so they could watch comets and see the rings of Saturn, and that's why his son was called Cepheus and his daughter was Lyra."

Ariel got the last of the seeds out. "I like it," she said. "Beats how I got my name."

Cassie gave her a sidelong look. A moment passed. Then she asked, "That movie?"

Ariel rolled her eyes and nodded.

"Could have been worse. Your folks might have watched *Dumbo* or something."

Ariel choked back a laugh. "Okay," she said. "Yeah, there's that. I'm fine with the name, though. I read Shakespeare's *The Tempest* for the first time when I was twelve and decided that was the Ariel I wanted to be named for."

"Nice," Cassie said, and then stopped and laughed. "And now that's exactly what you are, right? Your grandpa makes a pretty good Prospero."

Ariel's face lit up. "I didn't even think of that," she said, delighted. "And my mom would be *horrified*."

Cassie gave her another sidelong look, and another moment passed. "You know," she said then, "that's literally the first time you've mentioned that you even have a mom." With a grin: "I was starting to wonder if Dr. Moravec made you in a lab or something."

"Oh, I wish," said Ariel, meaning it. An image from an old movie came to mind; she bent one of her hands into a clawlike shape and raised it unsteadily from the table. "She lives! The monster lives!"

Thunder chose that moment to roll. Startled, both girls looked at the windows behind them, then laughed. "Yeah, I have a family," Ariel admitted. "They're in Summerfield. Mom calls me up once a week to yell at me because she doesn't like how I'm living my life. Dad never did do anything to stop her and I don't expect him to start now. My sister Britney's a snotnosed brat. I had a brother, Daniel, who was really nice, but ..." She shrugged, let the sentence trail off.

Cassie waited.

"He died in a car crash. This was like seven years ago." Seven years and four months, her memories reminded her. She silenced them before they counted out the days.

"Oh my God," Cassie said. "That *sucks*."

Ariel looked away, nodded. "Yeah."

A silence filled the room, and was promptly chased off by a flurry of rain drumming on the windows. Ariel turned her attention back to the angelica. After a little while, Cassie said, "If it's a problem that I asked about your family, I'm sorry."

Ariel glanced at her. "No, it's okay. It's just one of those things."

They both focused on the garbling for a while. Once the silence started to get oppressive, Ariel asked, "So how come Aunt Clarice isn't Aunt Ursa or something?"

Cassie choked with laughter. "Oh, *man*," she said. "That's good. But she was a Williams before she married my great-uncle Hercules. My sister and brothers and me are the only Jacksons who are part bear."

Ariel gave her an uncertain look.

"That's the story," Cassie said. "Way back when the first people came to Korea, there was this she-bear named Ungnye. She and a tiger decided they wanted to turn into people so they could help found Korea, and so they went to a cave to do spiritual stuff—fasting, praying, you know. The tiger couldn't hack it and ran off, but Ungnye kept at it night and day for twenty-one days, and finally the spirits decided she meant it and turned her into a beautiful maiden. So she went on down to the human city and Prince Hwanung, who came down from heaven to get Korea started, fell in love with her and married her. Their son was Dangun, who was the very first king of Korea, but the way my grandma Chung-hwae tells the story, they also had eight daughters, and every mudang family in Korea is descended from one of those daughters. So I'm part bear on my mom's side."

"Rowr?" Ariel asked.

"Rowr," said Cassie, with an enthusiastic nod.

Thunder rumbled again, further off. The rain flung one more handful of droplets at the windows and went away to sulk. "I knew Uncle Herk when I was little," Cassie said then. "He was really sweet to all us kids. He died when I was eight, and I cried and cried."

"I remember that well," said Aunt Clarice.

They both jumped. Once again, neither of them had heard the door open.

The old woman came over to the table and examined the piles of seeds, stems, and leaves. "Good," she said. "I'm going to have to interrupt your work for a little while, though. I've had a new client come in and ask for a reading, and I've got a feeling there'll be a few other people in the shop soon, before Tasha comes in. So I'll need you both to fill in behind the counter for a little while." To Ariel, who had been trying to keep her nervousness off her face: "No need to worry, child. Cassie'll show you what to do if there's need."

The three of them trooped out through the hallway and emerged in the shop. Aunt Clarice went back into the nook in back where she did her tea leaf readings. Cassie led Ariel over to the marble-topped counter near the window, waved her to a chair in the narrow space between counter and glass cases, and perched in another. "We'll have to keep it down," she said in not much more than a whisper. Clatter of tea being made further back in the shop, and murmur of low voices after that, explained why. "Unless somebody comes in—"

The front door opened with a jangle of bells, admitting a plump old woman with a biscuit-colored face, wearing a gray and white tweed coat and a plastic rain bonnet over an unconvincing blonde wig. She sent a vague smile toward the counter, made a beeline toward one of the shelves further in, and came to the counter with three odd little amulets in plastic packages. Cassie got up and said something polite, and the old woman came over and pulled money out of her purse. Ariel stood also, and watched closely as Cassie wrote up the purchase on an order pad, took the money, and handed back the change.

The old woman was scarcely out the door when a middle-aged black woman in a luminous blue raincoat came in, folded a dripping umbrella, and executed a close equivalent of the same process. Cassie wrote up her order and took her cash, too, making a little conversation in the process; Ariel gathered that they knew each other.

They were still busy when the door chimed again and a middle-aged man in a brown coat came in. Balding and red-faced, he had watery blue eyes that bulged out, giving him a popeyed look. He looked around uncertainly as soon as he was inside, then came straight over to the counter. Cassie was still busy with her customer, so Ariel gulped down her uncertainties, put on a smile, and said, "Can I help you?"

"I—yes, I hope so," the man said, sounding harried. His voice seemed just a little familiar to Ariel, though she wasn't sure why. "I need a shewstone—a crystal, you know, for scrying."

"Sure," said Ariel. The glass case behind her was well stocked with crystal balls of various sizes and materials, each supported by a little three-footed stand. "Anything particular?"

"Yes. It needs to be yellow, or, you know, gold colored."

Ariel went to the glass cases, the man at her heels. Three of the crystal balls there had a more or less yellowish color. She motioned at them, and the man said, "The one in the middle. I'd like to look at that if—if I could."

She got the ball out, took it back to the counter and set it there on its stand. It was a lovely golden color, she thought, a little smoky inside, and wondered what the man was planning to do with it. He bent down and examined it, nodding to himself and muttering in a low voice Ariel couldn't make out. "Yes," he said then, straightening up. "I—yes. Yes, this one will do."

"That'll be seventy-two dollars," said Ariel, who'd taken the necessary moment to read the little price sticker on it.

"Yes, of course. I—I hope you can take a credit card."

Ariel sent a panicked glance to Cassie. Fortunately the black woman in the vivid blue coat was heading toward the door just then. "Sure thing," Cassie said, and got a card reader from under the counter. "I can take care of that."

A glance under the counter showed Ariel where to find tissue paper and plastic shopping bags. She picked up the sphere, and found herself envying the customer; the crystal appealed to her, though she couldn't have explained why. Nonetheless she got it and its stand wrapped up promptly in paper and tucked into a plastic bag, and handed it over to the man, who babbled his thanks and then hurried out the door into the rain.

One more customer came in before Aunt Clarice finished giving her reading, a young black man in jeans and a leather jacket who leaned on the counter, chatted with Cassie, bought a High John the Conqueror root and made off. Maybe five minutes later the scrape of chairs in the back of the store announced the end of the divination; a grim-faced woman in an expensive wool coat hurried out, and Aunt Clarice emerged a few moments afterward, shaking her head. "Well," she said. "I hope it all comes out for the best." Cassie gave the old woman an uneasy look; Ariel, watching them both, wondered just how foreboding the divination had been.

The rest of the day was anticlimax, another hour or so of garbling angelica, followed by another hour listening to Aunt Clarice explaining just what could be done with the seeds, the stems, the leaves, and the roots of that herb. Ariel dutifully took down notes until her hand ached, and decided by the time the day was over that she was going to take a good hard look at the shorthand book she'd bought at the thrift store. Then Tasha Merriman arrived in a swirl of brightly colored clothing, teased Cassie, said something friendly to Ariel, handed Aunt Clarice a bag containing a late lunch from one of the restaurants down the street, and got ready for what promised to be a busy evening in the shop. Cassie and Ariel said their goodbyes and set out together up wet streets toward home.

The rain picked up again just after Cassie veered down March Street and kept at it until Ariel reached her grandfather's house, dousing her thoroughly. Once inside, her coat went onto the coat tree, where it started laying down a puddle on the entry floor, and Ariel went upstairs and changed into dry clothes. The stack of clippings about the prowler, perched on her desk, reminded her of questions she couldn't begin to answer. She went back downstairs, and only then found the note letting her know that her grandfather was busy with an important meeting at the Heydonian and wouldn't be back until late that night, and she was on her own for dinner.

A steaming cup of tea offered one consolation, and her usual corner of the sofa in the parlor provided another. She curled up, tried to convince herself to struggle through more of Eliphas Lévi, and failed. Instead, she picked up the older and thicker of the two books she'd gotten from the downtown library, *The Treasure of Captain Curdie, A Colonial Enigma* by Maude Gorton Wemberly, and plunged into it.

The ornate, rambling late-Victorian prose took a little while for her to get used to, but the effort was worth it. Where Delphinia Braddock had skimmed over the surface, Wemberly went deep. Her chronicle started with the founding of Adocentyn by Elias Ashmole and his occultist friends, traced the ancestors of Bartholomew Curdie to two islands off Scotland's west coast and a bitter era of poverty and political conflict, and brought the town and the family together deftly with an account of the ship that brought John and Isabel Curdie to Adocentyn and a new life in a burgeoning colony an ocean away from everything they'd known.

For a book nerd, as Ariel liked to think of herself, it was a fine way to spend an evening. Rain pattered on the windows, the three-dialed grandfather clock chimed the hours and a few other more exotic intervals, and the sky darkened; Ariel didn't notice until the room got so dark she could barely see the print on the pages. When that moment arrived, she got up long enough to turn on lights and close the curtains, took a sip of her tea, and made a face: it had gotten cold. She poured it down the kitchen sink, settled back on the sofa and kept reading.

More time passed. She didn't reach the first of the little scraps of white paper inside the book until she was more than halfway through, and trying to figure out what logic governed their placement added another mystery to the ones that already surrounded Captain Curdie and his treasure. She had passed four or five of them, leaving each one exactly in place, before she realized that they each marked a place where the book had something to say about Curdie's house in colonial Adocentyn. Thereafter she kept watch, nodding each time she found one and spotted the detail about the Curdie house it was meant to mark. Someone had gone through the book meticulously, she realized, and spotted every single passage that described the house.

By the time she turned the last page of the book the grandfather clock was striking ten. She set the volume aside and went out to the kitchen to fix something for dinner. A box of mac and cheese and a bowl of already-mixed salad from the fridge took care of that. She'd finished the meal, washed up the dishes, and started fixing tea before the familiar rattle of a key in the front door told her that Dr. Moravec had come home at last.

More sounds told of his coat and hat finding places on the coat tree. He came into the parlor looking vaguely disheveled as she came back out from the kitchen with two cups of tea, nodded a distracted greeting to her, then realized that one of the cups was for him and made a fractional bow to her before taking the cup. "Thank you," he said. "That's welcome just now, and not just on account of the weather."

"The meeting?"

"In a manner of speaking." He settled into his armchair, sipped tea. Then, to her surprise, he went on. "Theophilus Cray's return has ruffled a great many feathers. His great-great-grandfather, Erasmus Cray, put up a good fraction of the funds that built the Heydonian's present quarters, and kept his shares when others cashed out. Are you familiar with building societies of the old style? No? They sold shares to raise funds for construction, and then paid off the shares as funds permitted once the building was finished."

"And the Heydonian didn't pay everyone off?"

"It was a complex affair." A fractional shrug dismissed years of disputes. "The outcome is that the Board of Trustees owns just over sixty-two percent of the building and the remaining shareholders own the rest. Theophilus has the single largest block of shares, almost ten percent of the total. While he was gone he left his shares in a trust and gave the proxies to a committee of other shareholders. There's quite some question as to how closely they followed the instructions he gave them, and I gather that not all the shares have been accounted for."

Ariel took that in. "I hope you're not in any kind of trouble."

"Not at all. I wasn't on the Board of Trustees yet when he left. When a vacancy came up eight years later, one important reason I was elected was that I don't own shares myself, so there's no conflict of interest."

"Okay," said Ariel, nodding slowly.

"That's true of all of us on the Board—the bylaws require it—and so none of us was on the committee Theophilus set up, of course. But there'll be a certain amount of trouble for the institution if the whole business isn't cleared up promptly, and there's some disagreement about the right way to take care of it. Not the first time that's happened, of course."

Ariel nodded again. Dr. Moravec sipped tea and said nothing more. She watched him for a few minutes and then, knowing his moods, picked up Wemberly's book and headed upstairs to her bedroom.

She'd intended nothing more with the book than leaving it on the back corner of her desk where she put library books she meant to return, but a restless feeling made her sit down at her desk and flip idly through the pages again. The scraps of white paper caught her interest. She found them one at a time and took a close look at them. They all seemed to be torn from one edge of a sheet of ordinary white paper, they were all roughly the same length, and they hadn't been in the book long enough to pick up any of the brown tint from the pages. All but three were unmarked, and those three each had a scrap of black on one torn edge, as though the scraps were from the top of the sheet and something had been printed a little further down. Two of the marks were curved, like the very top of a capital letter C, G, O, or S; the third was a sharp little point that could only have been the top of a capital letter A.

That caught her attention. Memory surged up: a scrap of paper with a few stray marks on it had given her a crucial clue in the Criswell case. She stared at each of the scraps for a while, trying to figure out what they might have spelled out. That didn't get far, and after a while she put the book aside, got the volume of Dashiell Hammett stories out, and plunged into the first of a series of lively pulp detective tales.

All the while, though, another set of thoughts circled in the back of her mind. The book by Maude Gorton Wemberly wasn't in the online catalog, so the number of people who knew that it was there might be fairly small. One of them, not too long before, had taken the book seriously enough to mark the pages that might offer a hint to the location of Captain Curdie's treasure. Was it sheer coincidence that someone had recently prowled the streets where Curdie's estate had been?

She was still wrestling with the same question the day that Theophilus Cray came to visit.

CHAPTER 10

A WHISPER FROM ANTIQUITY

A riel had no warning of Cray's arrival. She'd left earlier than usual that morning for Aunt Clarice's shop, expecting nothing more than an ordinary day of learning the simpler kinds of magic, the sort of thing she could pick up without plunging ahead in her grandfather's wake. Aside from half an hour spent wolfing down a hastily packed lunch and wishing she knew how to make whatever delectably scented Korean rice-and-something dish Cassie was eating alongside her, she spent the whole day garbling half a dozen herbs and then mixing them together in certain strict proportions, following a recipe in Aunt Clarice's small neat handwriting on what looked like a scrap of brown paper grocery bag. The mix would protect against hostile magic and evil spirits, that much Aunt Clarice explained to her two pupils, and it could be put to work in a dozen ways, most of which the old woman didn't describe.

As the day wound down and heavy clouds came sweeping in to choke off the last of the daylight, Aunt Clarice had them each fill a little cloth bag with the mixture, tie it shut, and fasten it to a cord sized to fit around a neck, as a protective amulet—a toby, as the old woman called it. That was some compensation, but then Aunt Clarice gave them a somber look and saying, "I've got a feeling that one of you will need that before long."

That was unsettling, and it didn't help that Aunt Clarice told them both to take the next day off their studies—"Things are getting very serious," she said, "and I've got one reading after another scheduled tomorrow." Then, once Ariel and Cassie said their goodbyes and headed out the door into the damp chill of an autumn afternoon, Cassie proceeded to step hard on a different sore toe by bubbling over with enthusiasm about a ceremony she was going to help her mother perform for the local Korean-American community the next day. The contrast between the elaborate details of Cassie's training and the impenetrable wall Eliphas Lévi's prose seemed to be raising in front of Ariel made it an effort, and not a small one, to put on a smile and listen to Cassie's excited chatter. After they got to the corner of March Street and Green Avenue, and Cassie headed for home, Ariel's sour mood turned bitter, and she spent the remaining blocks kicking herself mentally for feeling jealous. All in all, it was not a pleasant walk.

The house on Lyon Avenue offered at least notional shelter from her thoughts, and she climbed the steps and let herself in the front door with relief. In place of the usual comforting hush, however, she heard voices from the parlor: her grandfather's deep voice, and then another, lighter, voice she almost recognized. She scowled, shed coat and shoulder bag, then forced a more pleasant expression on her face and went on into the parlor.

Her grandfather was sitting in his usual chair, and a teapot and cups she didn't recognize ornamented the coffee table. On the sofa, perched in Ariel's usual spot, was Theophilus Cray, in shirtsleeves and a red and black vest of unfamiliar cut. In place of the shapeless cap he'd worn to the bookshop, he had on a stiff flat-topped cap of felted red wool with curious metal ornaments on it; his white hair spilled irrepressibly out from underneath. He caught sight of her before her grandfather did, and beamed at her.

"Ariel," Dr. Moravec said then. "I believe you've met Theophilus Cray already."

"More or less," said Ariel, and to Cray: "Hi."

Cray got to his feet, extended a hand, bowed over hers in courtly fashion. "Good afternoon. I trust you'll forgive my very casual greeting a few days back; I'm sorry to say I have too much in common with the old man of Thermopylae, who never did anything properly."

Ariel gave him a blank look, then sent an uncertain glance toward her grandfather.

That response seemed to startle Cray. "Great heavens. Is it possible, child, that you haven't yet encountered the writings of the incomparable Edward Lear?"

"No," said Ariel, with another glance toward her grandfather, pleading.

Cray threw up his hands in a theatrical gesture of despair. "*O tempora! O mores!* Oh, what a world! What a life!" He turned to Dr. Moravec. In a minatory tone: "Bernard, you have shamefully neglected this poor girl's education."

Dr. Moravec met the accusation calmly. "She's only lived here for three months. Other pieces of remedial learning came first."

"Then her schoolteachers should be flogged!" Cray said, with another wild gesture.

By this point Ariel was beginning to wonder how best to extract herself from the parlor and flee to her room. That apparently communicated itself to Cray. Pale eyes glanced at her with a hint of amusement. "No, no, child, you mustn't mind me. I am older and stranger than I look, and not quite so silly. Yes, you may laugh. Please sit down and have a cup of tea."

Giving up any hope of escape, she let him pour her a cup of tea, went to sit in an armchair well away from him. His expression showed clearly enough that he'd noticed, and was amused by the action, but he turned to Dr. Moravec. "I trust you have a copy of Lear's collected nonsense somewhere in this house of yours."

"I still have the copy you gave me in 1988."

"Ah. Yes, that will do nicely. Well. Shall we resume our conversation, or would a different topic be more suitable?"

"Ariel," Dr. Moravec observed, "is my research and investigative assistant as well as my granddaughter. We can certainly continue."

Ariel sent him a grateful look, and tried a sip of the tea. It had an odd flavor, a little smoky, a little astringent. She tried another sip, decided she liked it. Meanwhile her grandfather said, "Theophilus has been out of the country, as you know. A decade or so after the Soviet Union collapsed, once it became possible for travelers from the West to visit certain isolated parts of Central Asia, he went searching for a place that most of us believed almost certainly didn't exist any more."

Cray chuckled. "So you thought, Bernard."

"I did indeed. So did nearly every scholar you consulted."

"And they were wrong. I never had any doubt of that." He raised his chin and chanted:

> "Higgledy-piggledy,
> Crazy Theophilus
> Got up one morning and
> Started to roam;
> Then he discovered a
> City of mystery,
> Boarded a freighter and
> Headed for home."

He turned to face Ariel. "Tell me this, my Jumbly Girl. Have you ever heard of Agharta?"

She shook her head and braced herself for the reaction, but the strange little man simply nodded. "Not surprising. I assure you, it's nowhere near the great Gromboolian plain or the towering heights of the hills of the Chankly Bore." He laughed, then tilted his head, observing her. "No, you really haven't read Lear, have you? Sad. Very sad. But Agharta is entirely real. During the last ice age, when the deserts of central Asia were green, when rain-fed lakes dotted what are now the Gobi and the Takla Makan deserts and forests wrapped the feet of the Tianshan Mountains, it was a city of considerable size."

Ariel gave him an uncertain look. "There were cities during the Ice Age?"

"They didn't teach you that in school, did they?" Cray waggled a finger in the air. "No, of course not. They taught you instead, I'm sure, that humanity sat around in caves twiddling its collective thumbs for a million years or so, and then suddenly leapt up a mere five thousand years ago and invented cities, writing, metalworking, astronomy, and the rest of it. Poppycock! In fact, balderdash! Does that fairy tale even make sense?"

"Well, no," Ariel admitted.

"Good. You are quite correct. It makes no sense at all. It is in fact pure hokum, propped up by nothing better than a simple refusal, on the part of official scholarship, to look at any evidence to the contrary. More tea, Bernard? Excellent. And you, my Jumbly Girl?"

She held out her cup, got a refill. "Why won't they look at the evidence?"

Cray beamed. "Good. Very good. You have a curious mind and you don't simply accept at face value the ravings of a strange old man." She choked back a laugh, and he waggled a finger at her. "No, no, you must let yourself laugh. It's quite unhealthy to stifle a laugh." Then, briefly serious: "History is dangerous stuff. If our ancestors twenty thousand years ago were grunting superstitious savages cowering in caves, that says one thing about who we are and what we can expect from the future. If they were urbane, civilized, literate, possessed of certain branches of knowledge we haven't yet equaled—why, that says something very different about both those things. Have you by any chance assisted Bernard in one of his investigations?"

Ariel sent a glance her grandfather's way, got a nod in response. "Yes, a couple of them."

"Excellent. This is the same sort of thing. Who stole the priceless jewel? It depends a very great deal on who did or did not have access to that end of the mansion on the night when it vanished. A matter of history, in quite a literal sense."

"You might be interested to know," said Dr. Moravec then, "that a priceless jewel has in fact been stolen: the Denby-Adams shewstone."

Cray looked up at him. Every trace of levity had vanished from his face. "Has it indeed. Are there suspects?"

"Not to my knowledge. It was reported missing the day you returned."

A momentary silence passed. "I wish I could say I was surprised. Well."

"One of several curious events in the last few days," Dr. Moravec went on. "I wonder. Do you know of a late medieval or early modern Latin grimoire, central or eastern European origin, with a name approximating *Liber Nathan*?"

Cray's eyebrows drew together. "No," he said after another pause. "No, I don't believe I've heard of such a thing."

Dr. Moravec considered that, nodded. "It seemed worth asking. A local family owned it until some time in the last month or so, when it vanished. I was called in, of course."

"Of course. *Liber Nathan*." He frowned again, and finally shook his head. "No. Though it's been a few years since I last concerned myself with anything so recent. Doubtless I'm slipping. Any other mysterious appearances or disappearances? No? Why, I'm disappointed, Bernard. Sorely disappointed."

He turned back to Ariel, and as though nothing else had been brought up, went on in the same jocose vein as before: "So you see there was quite a bit of importance to my little quest.

And of course I couldn't simply go strolling out into the deserts of central Asia and expect to find Agharta. That's been tried, quite a few times now, and not everyone who tried it came back alive. Oh, dear me, no, not by any measure."

"Ossendowski survived the experience," said Dr. Moravec. "Barely."

"He did indeed." To Ariel: "Ferdinand Ossendowski escaped Russia the hard way after the Communists won the Russian Civil War. He went on foot through the heart of central Asia, and brought back some very remarkable stories. Some other travelers did the same. Nicholas Roerich probably got closer to Agharta than anyone else, back before the Iron Curtain came down and it was worth more than your life to venture into that part of the world. Not just for Westerners, either. The Soviets and the Chinese lost people as well. You might have heard of the Dyatlov Pass incident—it's received some press even in this country."

Ariel, uncertain, shook her head.

"No? A party of experienced Russian hikers, found dead in the snow in mysterious circumstances. Not all the bodies were intact, and some were radioactive. You might look it up sometime. But as you see, I am quite alive, and I don't yet glow in the dark. I was more cautious and more patient. I settled in Irkutsk, on the shores of Lake Baikal. I had already learned to speak Russian and Mongolian quite fluently, and picked up a working knowledge of the languages of the nearby Siberian tribes. People in Irkutsk got used to my presence. They called me—no, we can let that pass, every second word in ordinary conversational Russian is a profanity."

Ariel choked. Cray gave her an amused look, and went on. "I gathered information, made friends, won the trust of certain shamans—that's the homeland of shamanism, you know, the place the word 'shaman' came from—and finally reached my goal. Not, mind you, Agharta." He waggled a finger. "That would have gotten me killed, no matter what preparations I had made. The old Brotherhoods guard their secrets far, far better than that."

"Brotherhoods?" Ariel asked.

"Oh, yes. There are several of them, and they've been around for a very long time. The oldest, quite possibly since Aghartan times. Others are more recent, if you call four or five thousand years recent. They keep watch on the ruins of Agharta and make good and sure that no one goes there without some highly appropriate reason. I had no desire to risk their wrath. So I simply waited, and let it be known that I was interested in certain things, and eventually one of the Brotherhoods sent someone to talk to me."

"The Sarmoung?" Dr. Moravec asked him.

"Oh, good heavens, no. The Sarmoung Brotherhood's much more standoffish than that. How Gurdjieff managed to get admitted to their chief monastery still baffles me. No, it was the Qimbalang, as I thought it would be."

"Ah," said Dr. Moravec. Ariel gave him a startled look; the monosyllable seemed to be freighted with meaning, though what it meant was wholly opaque to her.

"Exactly," said Cray, as though he'd grasped every detail in the word. "I'm pleased to say they were just as hospitable to me as they were to Paracelsus all those years ago. Of course I couldn't hope to get them to take me to the ruins of Agharta itself, but they allowed me to stay at one of their monasteries for quite a number of years and study certain very old records, and they gave me the chance to visit two other sites where I was able to inspect ruins from Aghartan times. As you might expect, I had some remarkable adventures in the process."

"I think we'll both want to hear about those," Dr. Moravec said. "First, though, I should ask whether we can offer you dinner."

"Oh, *au contraire*, Bernard! Is it possible that Trattoria Udine is still in existence?"

"Not only possible but quite certain. Federico retired ten years ago but Marcia—you recall her, of course? Good. Yes, she's in charge now, and the food hasn't suffered at all from the change. Quite the opposite, in fact."

"Excellent. Permit me to invite you to dinner." He turned toward Ariel. "I trust you'll allow me to make that a party of three. I promise you that the serious drinking won't begin until after we've returned here."

The thought of her grandfather drinking more than his very occasional snifter of brandy startled Ariel, though she kept her reaction off her face. She considered the options, decided to take the risk. "Sure," she said. "Thank you."

Dr. Moravec got up. "I'll call ahead. Marcia deserves fair warning."

"Indeed she does. I dated her more than once."

Dr. Moravec gave him a slightly glazed look. "I wasn't aware of that."

"No? I suppose neither of us was interested in trumpeting the details of our amours from the rooftops. I trust she's happily married now, with half a dozen squalling brats—no, they'd be turning out squalling brats of their own by now, wouldn't they?"

"Married," said Dr. Moravec, "and divorced. I'll tell you the story another time."

He vanished into the kitchen, and promptly enough Ariel heard his deep voice saying something she couldn't make out into the telephone. In his absence, Cray considered her. "No, my Jumbly Girl, you really mustn't mind me," he said. "Partly because your grandfather's a very dear friend of mine and I look forward to spending time with him again after all these years, but partly for your own sake. Bernard has told me a little about how you came here this summer and why you stayed, and that cheered me, since the manner in which I left home was not entirely dissimilar. I'll tell you the story someday. But I assure you there's more to your moving here and staying here than you know. Why, there's more to it than I know, and I know a very great deal. I won't try to guess what might be caught up in it all, not yet, but I have a suspicion that you and I will have to get used to each other's company."

Flustered, Ariel considered him. He beamed at her, turned to face the kitchen door as Dr. Moravec came back through it.

"Marcia's been duly forewarned," he said, "and a table for three will be waiting in fifteen minutes. Shall we?"

Ariel stifled her uncertainties, put on a smile and got to her feet.

CHAPTER 11

A THREAD OF CONNECTION

The restaurant was a little place only a block from the lighthouse on Lambspring Point, nestled into a two-story brick house of early twentieth-century vintage. A parking space for the Buick opened up a few blocks away. From there, Ariel followed her grandfather and Theophilus Cray along the sidewalk, half listening to their conversation, half looking at the neighborhood and the tall white spire of the lighthouse rising up over the roofs nearby, until they climbed the steps to the front door and went inside.

By the time Ariel got through the door, Marcia Degano had already come bustling into the entry to greet them. A plump black-haired woman in her middle years, wearing a billowing flower-print dress in garish reds and greens, she was both the proprietress and the hostess; she fussed over Dr. Moravec, greeted Cray with an affectionate reserve that made Ariel think there might still be unfinished business between them, welcomed Ariel with a broad smile and elaborate courtesies, and led them further in.

A dozen small tables crowded into what had once been the parlor and dining room, and swinging doors let into the kitchen. Marcia led them to a table at the far end of the dining room and waved them to the chairs. As they sat, she exchanged a few sentences with Cray in a language that sounded almost like Italian but not quite, and headed off to say something in the same language to the elderly couple at a table nearby.

Ariel's tentative question fielded, as she expected, a lively response from Theophilus Cray. "Friulian!" he said, as though the word would conjure up something from the tablecloth. "The dialect of the far northeast corner of Italy. Lovely country, very mountainous, and the culture and cuisine's as influenced by the Slavic countries to north and east as it is by anything more stereotypically Italian. There are remarkable traditions there, things that have been going on practically unchanged since the early Middle Ages. It's been a good long while, but I learnt the language, and spent two years there looking for certain things."

Ariel guessed that asking what the certain things were wouldn't get her far, and let the question lapse. She had more than enough to keep her attention occupied. The food was very good indeed, from the fresh-baked bread and olive oil and the salad straight through to the *gulash Triestino* she'd chosen mostly at random for her main course. She gathered from a comment of Marcia's that if she'd asked for wine she would have gotten it, but she wasn't feeling quite that daring just then. Instead, she sipped sparkling water, enjoyed the meal, and did much more listening than talking.

She did not lack for entertainment. Cray hadn't been exaggerating when he said he had had remarkable adventures, and he was as good a storyteller as Ariel had ever encountered. His hands and his voice did an impressive job of conjuring up the vast deserts and soaring mountains of central Asia, and he had a habit of breaking up the more serious parts of his story with little amusing anecdotes, mostly at his own expense. Serious parts there were, for the unseen center of it all was Agharta, an abandoned city 20,000 years old huddled on the shore of a long-vanished lake, its weathered ruins more than half smothered with windblown sand, guarded from intruders by secretive Brotherhoods and by other things, about which Cray gave only hints. Even the smaller and less important ruins that he had visited were risky to approach, and he'd barely escaped with his life on more than one occasion.

It was heady stuff. After the meal was over, they took their leave of Marcia and filed out the door, and Ariel wondered for a moment if the waiter had slipped a little alcohol into her water without saying a word about it, her thoughts were that jumbled. The whole way home, looking out the window of the back seat as Dr. Moravec drove, she brooded over what Cray had said about lost cities and Ice Age civilizations, and briefly imagined herself venturing into the wilds of Siberia to try to talk to one of the Brotherhoods. Reality sank in promptly, and she shook her head and watched the buildings move past.

Once they'd returned to the house on Lyon Avenue and coats festooned the coat tree in the entry, Cray turned to her and said, "Now the serious drinking begins. Consider yourself given fair warning."

She didn't stifle the laugh. "Okay, got it. Time for me to take the bounce."

Cray gave her a startled look, and then bowed. "My grandmother Florinda used to say that very thing on occasion. My Jumbly Girl, you've managed the not inconsiderable feat of making me feel young again. Thank you."

Ariel managed a more or less adequate curtsey in response, said her goodnights to them both, and headed up the stair to her room. Once the door clicked shut behind her and the quiet of the night closed in, she crossed to her bed, where Nicodemus the stuffed wolf waited with his usual patience. She rumpled the synthetic fur on his head, then remembered one of Cray's stories about Siberian wolves: they ran in big packs, he'd said, and now and then chased down and killed people. That sent a shiver down her back. She gave Nicodemus an uneasy look and went to her desk to read for a while before bed.

The clippings she'd gathered about the prowler still waited on the corner of the desk. The thought of pirate treasure, if that was in fact what the prowler was looking for, seemed almost bland next to age-old forgotten cities half buried in the sands of distant deserts. She reminded herself that the shortage of hungry wolf packs on the streets of Adocentyn was an advantage worth having, and buried herself in one of F. Scott Fitzgerald's stories until she was too sleepy to follow the sparkling Jazz Age prose any further.

The next morning she woke to the sound of rain drumming on the windows. Heavy gray clouds blotted out more than half the daylight, and the downtown skyline stood dim and drear behind veils of mist. The clippings about the prowler still sat on the corner of the desk, and brought back a flurry of questions she still couldn't answer.

Once she'd showered and dressed, she went downstairs expecting a few hours of solitude, but light shone yellow and cheerful in the kitchen. She went through the doorway to find Theophilus Cray perched on one of the kitchen chairs, sipping from one of her grandfather's teacups. Whatever was in it, it smelled of strange herbs rather than any kind of tea she knew.

"Good morning," he said, beaming up at her.

She repeated the phrase, got the coffee maker started, then stopped halfway to the toaster. "Do you want some toast, or—"

"No, no." A gesture with one hand waved away the suggestion. "I never eat before noon. One of my oddities. I don't recommend it to anyone else. By all means proceed."

Ariel didn't argue. Once the toast was in and the coffee maker had begun to clear its throat, she turned uncertainly toward the table. The old man glanced up from his teacup, waved her over. "Oh, please sit down. I may have helpful advice for you."

She sat facing him. "Okay."

"It's quite simple. You're perplexed by something. I can tell. You were far too polite to intrude it into yesterday evening's very pleasant conversation, but it's very much on your mind this morning. Am I right?"

Startled, she managed a nod. "Yeah."

"Tell me your perplexity." A hand went up, stopping her before she could begin. "Not the details. Summarize. Abstract. What is the shape of it?"

That took time, and more mental effort than she expected. Finally she said, "There are two things going on. No, there are three. I think they're all connected but I can't tell if I'm right, and if there's a connection I can't tell what it is."

"Good." Theophilus set down his cup and folded his hands together, the long thin fingers twining around each other in an odd way. "Very good." Pale eyes turned toward hers, but they didn't focus on her, or on anything else in the kitchen. "Yes, there's a connection. Yes, you can find it, but you won't find it in any way that makes logical sense. Feel free to doubt that."

"No," said Ariel. "I don't know much about magic but I know it's not logical."

"Do you? Better still." The pale eyes turned her way again. "Listen carefully, for I don't repeat myself when it comes to important things. I'll be leaving here in a matter of moments. After I've left, go into the parlor, close your eyes, turn around three times clockwise and as much more as feels right, and then open your eyes. Pick up the first book you see. Let it fall open to whatever page the Fates choose. Look down that page for a word. One word, my Jumbly Girl. Your eye will light upon it, you will know that it's the word you need, and if you think it over you will understand why. Now repeat what I've just told you, as exactly as you can."

She repeated it back to him.

"Excellent." He drained the last of the teacup, got up, set it in the sink, and turned to her. "It may be some little while before we see each other again. I was gone a good deal longer than I originally intended, and the arrangements I made to see that things were taken care of in my absence turned out to be far less adequate than I'd hoped. If days and weeks and months pass, and you wonder whatever happened to the funny little man who visited your grandfather, don't think that you've been forgotten. We'll speak again in due time, and when we do, it's quite possible that I'll have something to say that you'll find very interesting indeed." He bowed, crossed the kitchen, waved her back to her seat when she started to rise. "No, no, I'll let myself out. Like the aquatic old person of Grange, my manners are scroobious and strange." Looking past her at the window as another volley of raindrops beat against it: "And his waterproof tub would be decidedly useful just now. Oh, well. He isn't here, and in a moment or two, I won't be here either. Farewell, my Jumbly Girl."

"Goodbye," she said, and listened to the rustle of his coat as he put it on and the whisper and click of the front door as he closed it on the way out.

Once he was gone, she got her toast and coffee, finished them, and went out into the parlor, meaning to go to the front door and rescue the newspaper. Only then did she recall the odd instructions Cray had given her. They seemed ludicrous, but she shrugged and decided to follow them. Standing in the middle of the parlor, she closed her eyes, spun around until she was sure she'd gone around more than three times, stopped and opened her eyes. She was facing the end table on her end of the sofa, and the first book she saw was Eliphas Lévi's *Dogme et Rituel de la Haute Magie.*

She stifled a groan, but made herself go pick it up. The book fell open in her hand to a page close to the end, and she found herself looking at the list of spirits she'd noticed earlier. She ran her finger down the page, past spirit after spirit, until her eye caught on one entry:

HAATAN, génie qui cache les trésors

She translated it at a glance as "Haatan, spirit that hides treasures." That seemed promising, but what did it have to do with the masked prowler, or the missing book, or the stolen shewstone? She set Lévi's book down again and went to the front door to get the newspaper.

Outside rain drummed down on the sidewalk and the stair. Ms. Pawelik had stuffed the paper into a flimsy plastic bag and tucked it up close to the door, as she always did on rainy days, but the end closest to the opening was wet anyway. Ariel scooped up the paper, shook the rain off the bag, and fled back inside. She was most of the way to the kitchen table when the name of the spirit murmured itself again in her thoughts: Haatan.

She stopped, then went the rest of the way into the kitchen. The newspaper went onto the table, more coffee found its way into her cup, the scissors and the list of topics her grandfather had written out for her made their appearance, and all the while the name hovered in her mind. Around it, very slowly, the world took on a different shape. Just as Theophilus Cray had promised, the prowler, the book, and the shewstone all became part of a single pattern, and the name of a spirit was the thread of connection that linked them.

She got up from the table, hurried up to her room, found a notebook and spent five minutes writing, so she wouldn't forget any of the details. Then, more slowly, she came back downstairs to the kitchen, settled at the table, sipped coffee, and went to work harvesting the day's clippings.

More than two hours passed before she heard the whisper of Dr. Moravec's footsteps on the stair. By then she'd long since finished with the paper. The clippings had found their way to the corner of his study desk, and she was curled up on the sofa, Eliphas Lévi's book in her hands. She was still struggling with it, but the French had gotten easier with daily practice, and some of what the old mage discussed had started to make sense. Will and imagination, he said, were the keys to magic: imagine your purpose richly and will it powerfully, and the astral light, whatever that was, would flow into the pattern thus formed and turn imagination into reality. That didn't quite make sense to her, but it came closer to making sense than most of what she'd read.

She had just finished brooding over this when the first footsteps sounded. She wondered, as they got louder, what effect a night of serious drinking might have had on her grandfather. A moment later she was relieved to have the answer: none that she could see. He nodded to her as usual, went into the kitchen, and produced the usual noises. Just over seven minutes later he was back out with his invariable breakfast.

"Good morning," he said. "I gather Theophilus is gone."

"Yeah. He was up when I came downstairs. We talked a little and then he left. He said it would probably be a while before I saw him again."

Dr. Moravec settled in his usual chair, got plate and cup settled. "Yes, he cautioned me about that. Doubtless I'll see him at the Heydonian sooner or later." He speared a piece of kipper with his fork.

Ariel gathered up all her courage and asked, "Do some books of sorcery teach how to call up spirits to find treasure?"

The old man's eyebrows went up. "Yes," he said after a moment. "Yes, in fact, those were quite popular once upon a time, especially in Europe and America. In the days before banks, when one of the few ways to keep large amounts of money safe was to hide it underground, a good many people used magic to try to find buried treasure. The most common way was to call spirits into a shewstone and get them to reveal where treasure was hidden. The Heydonian has quite a collection of treasure-hunting manuals in its closed stacks, and a fair number of shewstones in the museum. Why?"

"Mr. Cray had a suggestion for me." She explained what he'd told her, and what she'd done. "And the word I found was the name of Haatan, the spirit that hides treasures."

He paused, and then set his fork down. "Haatan. Of course."

"You see it, don't you?" Ariel said. "The Kozlowskis' book isn't the *Book of Nathan* or anything else. It's the *Book of Haatan*.

Somebody stole it to try to use magic to find Captain Curdie's treasure. Maybe the same person stole Elias Ashmole's shew-stone to use with the book. And the same person might be the one who was prowling around this part of the city with a mask on. I bet he was looking for traces of Curdie's house."

"A prowler," said Dr. Moravec. "I don't think that's been mentioned to me." He picked his fork up again and went back to work on breakfast.

Ariel blushed. "I didn't think it had anything to do with the book. Aunt Clarice told me about the prowler the first day I started studying with her, and Cassie—" It occurred to her then that she hadn't mentioned Cassie at all to her grandfather. "Cassie Jackson, her great-niece, who she's also teaching. She heard about the prowler too. I started clipping reports from the paper, and everyone who saw him said he was in the part of town that used to be the Curdie estate."

"Which you've looked up."

"At the downtown library. I was curious."

Dr. Moravec nodded, and sipped coffee. "A useful habit." He was silent for a while. Ariel waited. "I think," he said finally, "it's worth pursuing this. I can make some inquiries, and then—" He paused, went on. "Then, I think, we can take a risk or two."

Abruptly he changed the subject. "What did you think of Theophilus?"

Ariel thought about that for a moment. "He was right," she said. "He's stranger than he looks, and not as silly as he likes to pretend."

"Good. Yes on both counts." He finished the last of his breakfast and washed it down with coffee. "Theophilus is an odd duck even for Adocentyn. He grew up in a very rich family, one of the richest in the state. You've doubtless seen the kind of doting mothers who treat their children like china dolls and insist that they can't possibly stand a moment's strain. His was like that. So the day he turned eighteen he walked down to the recruiting station and signed up for the Marine Corps."

Ariel stared. "Seriously?"

"Very much so. By the time his mother found out he was already at boot camp. He served his four years as a rifleman, saw combat in I forget which small war, and got an honorable discharge. He told me later that he wanted to find out if he really was as fragile as his mother insisted. Myself, I think he knew perfectly well already, and wanted to make a point his mother couldn't ignore."

"It's kind of what I did."

"You can be sure he's well aware of that. We talked a little about you."

She blushed, but said, "He mentioned that. He also said he thinks we're going to have to get used to each other."

"Yes, he mentioned that to me also. I suspect he's right, for what it's worth."

Ariel pondered that for a few moments. "Will it help if I read Edward Lear?"

"It might. On the other hand, it's quite possible that he'll be quoting something else when we next see him." The old man gathered up plate and cup, got up and carried them toward the kitchen. In the doorway, he stopped and turned back toward her. "Do you think you could find time to take another note to Dupois & Company sometime in the next day or two?"

"Sure. Aunt Clarice said she's going to be swamped with clients all day, so I can go this afternoon if you want."

"Excellent. If you're right about the Kozlowskis' book, Genevieve Dupois ought to be able to set things in motion, and then—" He allowed a precise smile. "Then we'll see what the thief does about it." He turned and went into the kitchen.

CHAPTER 12

A GAMBLE WORTH TAKING

The Dupois & Company bookshop hadn't gotten any less crammed with books when Ariel stepped through the door. Some of the stacks of books on the floor seemed to have moved, and she didn't think most of the volumes heaped on the sales counter were the same ones that had been there when she'd visited earlier, but in the vast profusion of books it hardly mattered. She looked around, tried to guess where a clerk might be hiding.

A moment passed, and then one emerged from between two shelves further back in the store. It was the same young man she'd seen there earlier, the one with the single unbroken eyebrow. He had an armload of dusty hardback books. He looked startled to see her, but took the books to the sales counter, found a place to stack them, and said, "Can I help you?" as though he meant it this time.

"Please," said Ariel. "I've got another message for Ms. Dupois."

"Just a moment." He headed back and vanished somewhere in among the shelves.

Minutes passed. Lacking anything else to do, Ariel wandered over to the sales counter and considered the books there. Most of them were still in languages she didn't know, but right on top of the stack the young man had brought out was an old paperbound volume in French titled *Amphithéatre des Sciences Morts: Comment On Devient Mage*. "How to become a mage" sounded promising, though "amphitheater of dead sciences" was more unnerving. She picked up the book, opened it at random. The first sentence she saw translated promptly enough in her mind: *Fear the example of others, think for yourself. This precept of Pythagoras contains all of magic, which is nothing other than the power of selfhood.* That intrigued her; she turned back to the title page and then to the portrait of the author a few pages on, and wondered who Joséphin Péladan had been and what had put the haunted, haggard look into his face.

Low sounds in the back of the store let her know that someone was coming back, and she closed the book and put it down hastily. The young man emerged again. "She'll be out in a couple of minutes." Then, diffidently: "Mrs. Dupois said that you're Dr. Moravec's granddaughter. You're new in town?"

"Yeah. I moved here three months ago."

He nodded, as though she'd confirmed something. "A weird place, right? Adocentyn takes some getting used to."

"You're from here?"

A quick shake of his head denied it. "My folks moved here when I was twelve. We used to live in St. Quentin, if you know where that is."

"Not really," she admitted.

"About forty miles north of here, right on the coast. I still kind of miss it."

"Well, then you're lucky. I grew up in Summerfield and I don't miss it at all."

He opened his mouth to answer, then caught the sound of movement further back in the store, closed his mouth and got busy sorting the books he'd brought to the sales counter. Ariel stifled a grin and turned toward the sound.

Genevieve Dupois came into sight a moment later. She'd changed the black skirt for a navy blue one and her severe white blouse had a slightly different cut, but her expression still had all the warmth of a glacier. She greeted Ariel with a precise "Good afternoon, Ms. Moravec," took the sealed envelope Ariel offered her, thanked her, and went back out of sight. Ariel watched her go, then said goodbye to the clerk and left the shop. She could feel the clerk's gaze following her, and wondered briefly about that before other thoughts pushed that one aside.

The rest of the day was anticlimax. If Dr. Moravec had set anything in motion by the note, or whatever other steps he might have taken, the results didn't show themselves to Ariel. Back home, she wrestled with a chapter of Lévi's book, brooded over the words she'd read in the book by Péladan, and then fled from the whole subject into one of her favorite Somerset Maugham novels and spent the evening agreeably that way.

The next day was Saturday. All that morning, as she fixed her breakfast, clipped articles from the *Adocentyn Mercury*, settled down to try to make sense of another chapter of *Dogme et Rituel de la Haute Magie*, and stared out the window at leaves flying past in a brisk wind, Ariel kept a wary eye turned toward the telephone. Given the way the previous call had ended, she knew, it was anybody's guess whether her mother would call that week at all. If she did call, it was anybody's guess what she would say. None of that helped Ariel's mood any.

She spent fragments of the morning trying to come up with something she could say to get her mother to stop harping on the college education and the corporate job that she knew in her bones she didn't want. None of her attempts got far, and finally she filed the whole question for future reference and threw all of her effort into trying to make sense of what Eliphas Lévi had to say about magical equilibrium.

She had gotten only a few paragraphs into the chapter when the phone rang. The temptation to leave it unanswered was strong, but she shoved that aside, made herself go out into the kitchen and pick up the phone. "Hello?"

"Hello, Ariel? It's Teresa Kozlowski. You said I should call when I had time to offer you that cup of coffee."

Ariel found herself fumbling through a response, because the voice sounded almost as though it belonged to a different woman. The tired and half-defeated tone had vanished as if it had never been, replaced by a bubbling cheerfulness. Something had happened, Ariel was certain, but what?

They settled on a time that afternoon. Half an hour beforehand, Ariel got her purse and a jacket warm enough to deal with the wind and headed out into the Culpeper Hill neighborhood. The streets seemed even emptier and shabbier than usual, as though the autumn was turning them brown and withered along with the leaves. The thought that a pirate's treasure might be hidden somewhere in among the earnest middle-class homes and the rundown apartments of the working poor seemed hopelessly absurd, and she wondered whether the masked prowler's quest and the theft of the book and the shewstone had turned out to be futile efforts after all.

The porch of the Kozlowski house still sagged, and the same air of weary poverty still clung to the yard and the street. Ariel knocked on the door and waited. After a minute or so the door opened and Lucy looked out. "Oh, hi," she said, grinning. "Come in." As Ariel stepped into the entry, the girl turned toward the living room and called out, "Mom? It's Ariel."

"Oh!" said Teresa, clearly embarrassed. Then, to Ariel's surprise, a male voice she didn't recognize said something in a genial tone.

Lucy waved her into the parlor and then trotted up the stair. After a moment's hesitation, Ariel went on in. Teresa was there, perched on the sofa, and a stocky man in jeans and a flannel shirt sat across from her in an armchair. "I'm so sorry, Ariel," Teresa said, blushing. "I completely lost track of time. This is Phil Benedetti, the builder I called in to fix the leak in the bathroom. Phil, this is Ariel Moravec."

Ariel went over to greet him, and he got up and gave her his hand. It was easily twice the size of hers, muscled and callused. "Pleased to meet you." Then, to Teresa: "I can head on out now if you want."

"I won't mind if you finish your coffee first," said Ariel, who'd spotted the mostly full cup on the end table next to him.

He beamed and sat back down. "Thank you kindly."

Teresa got to her feet. "A cup for you, Ariel? Sugar, cream? Give me just a moment." She went into the kitchen.

Ariel sized up Phil Benedetti as quickly as she could. Black hair with a hint of gray at the temples framed a square homely face. The first few wrinkles at the corners of eyes and mouth suggested that he smiled often. Jeans and shirt were clean but showed signs of hard wear, and his lace-up boots showed their share of scars. Trying to make conversation, she said, "You and Teresa go to the same church, right?"

He beamed again. "Yeah. You wouldn't expect an Italian guy like me to go to the Polish Catholic Church, right? I used to go to Blessed Sacrament on North Hill, but the priests there did some things—" He gave his head a quick little shake, like a cat trying to get water off its fur. "We don't have to get into what. I walked out and stayed out, and that was kind of hard, since I started going to Mass every Sunday when I was a kid, you know? But a guy who works for me, name of Mike Pilsudski, told me about St. Adalbert's, said it was Catholic but not Roman. So I went with him the Sunday afterwards, and never looked back."

Teresa came back into the room, handed Ariel a cup of coffee. "We were all pleased to see him even at first," she said, "but he's been doing repairs on the church building and helping out people in the congregation who need it."

"Least I could do," said Phil. "A guy's gotta keep busy, right? And most of it's pretty easy jobs, too."

"I hope the problem with the plumbing here wasn't too bad," said Ariel.

Phil shook his head. "Not the plumbing part. One of the slip joint nuts for the sink drain in the upstairs bath worked itself loose. For all I know one of the kids monkeyed with it or something, but it let a bunch of water go down through the wall. The pipes took about fifteen minutes to fix. The wall, now that was another matter. You get water into old plaster, it's a mess. I had to tear it out and put in some new wallboard." He finished his coffee. "Well, why don't I leave you two to talk? Pleasure meeting you, Ms. Moravec." He turned to Teresa, sent a big smile her way. "Give me a call later today, will you?"

"Of course I will," Teresa said, with an even more luminous smile.

He said his goodbyes and headed out. By then Ariel was already sure she knew what had happened to change Teresa's state of mind, but decided to put it to the test and said, "He seems like a really nice person."

The smile she got in response annihilated any remaining doubt. "Oh, yes. I don't know why I never got around to talking to him before, since we go to the same church and everything. You remember the day you helped me get the yarn home, and I found out about the plumbing, right? I worked up the nerve to call him right after you left, and he was just so friendly, and came over right away. He got everything fixed the next day, but we got to talking, and he's come over half a dozen times since then, and—"

Ariel let her chatter on, knowing it would be a waste of time to try to turn the conversation toward anything but Phil Benedetti. She remembered plenty of conversations in high school with friends who were crazy in love, and recognized the same signs in Teresa's face and voice. An occasional question on her part was all that was required. It didn't take much imagination to come up with the right questions, either.

"Oh, Lucy and Joey both adore him," said Teresa, after Ariel had asked about her family's reaction. "His wife died seven years ago, she was pregnant with their first—it was really sad,

I teared up when he told me about it—and he loves kids but of course he doesn't have any of his own. The thing that surprised me was Paul. He hasn't always been too happy when I've talked about maybe trying to meet other guys someday and start dating. I used to tease him and tell him he was being jealous. But he says he likes Phil, and when I told him I wanted to marry Phil, he said he was fine with it."

"Do you think Phil's going to pop the question soon?"

Teresa nodded excitedly. "I think so. I really think so. Yesterday and then today he said some things and asked some questions that reminded me so much of the way that poor Alex edged around things before he asked me to marry him." She suddenly started blinking back tears. "After Alex died I thought I'd never be able to love anyone again. But it's been four years now, and literally the moment I met Phil I knew that I'd been wrong."

Ariel had already spotted the box of tissues on an end table. She got up, brought Teresa the box, sat down again. Teresa beamed at her through the tears, dabbed at her eyes with a tissue and said, "Thank you. I know I shouldn't get all worked up this way, but—" A helpless shrug punctuated the sentence.

That led promptly enough to another monologue about Phil Benedetti's virtues. Halfway through it, Paul came down the stairs and into the parlor, moving slowly, leaning on his cane. "Oh, excuse me," he said. "Teresa, got any idea where Lucy might have put one of my library books? It's got a green cover."

"Right there," said Teresa, pointing to one of the end tables. "Do I need to talk to her?"

"Probably." He went over and picked up a book. It had, Ariel noted, a cloth binding, and though the quick glimpse she got of the words on the back didn't communicate much, she was sure they had been stamped into the cloth binding. "Hi, Ariel. Any word?"

Ariel shook her head. "We're still waiting to hear from the booksellers."

He nodded, gave her a wan smile, and picked his way back to the entry and the stair. The moment he was gone, Teresa started talking about Phil Benedetti again, as Ariel expected. Once that ran down, she asked Teresa a question about their church, and that got an unexpected reaction. "We'd love to welcome you and your grandfather there, you know. Here—" Teresa turned to the nearest end table, found a few sheets of paper stapled together. "This is the church bulletin—it's got the times of services and everything."

Ariel took it and glanced at it. The words St. Adalbert's Church ran along the top of the first page, and the text below and on the following pages covered all the usual details: upcoming events, times and dates for Mass and catechism classes, a sermonette on why saying the Rosary was important, and an update on the church's fundraising efforts, written in a tone of forced optimism that failed to hide the very modest sums the church had obtained and the rising burden of deferred maintenance that had to be covered.

"I'll talk to him about it," Ariel promised, and put the bulletin into her shoulder bag.

"Would you? That would be so nice." Teresa looked up at the clock on the wall, then, and said, "Oh, dear. I should be getting dinner started soon."

"And you should give Phil a call, too" said Ariel, and stifled a smile when Teresa blushed bright pink.

A minute or two later, Ariel went down the steps and set out for Lyon Avenue. The wind had picked up and dark gray clouds scudded overhead. She huddled into her jacket and hurried through mostly empty streets, hoping to get home before another round of rain began to fall. A first few drops came down hard on the sidewalk when she was a block from safety, but the rest held off until she was safely inside.

She caught the sound of voices from the parlor as soon as she closed the door. Once her jacket was on the coat tree next to an unfamiliar brown raincoat, she paused, uncertain. Then she heard her grandfather say, "I'm sorry I can't be of more help," and a higher-pitched voice that seemed just slightly familiar said, "Thank you anyway. I—I appreciate your time."

That was close enough to an all clear that she decided to risk going into the parlor, if only to get to the kitchen and a cup of something hot to drink. As she came through the doorway, Dr. Moravec was rising to his feet, and so was a middle-aged man in a brown tweed jacket and tan slacks. Balding and red-faced, he had watery blue eyes that bulged slightly and a face lined with worry. It took Ariel only a moment to recognize him as the man who had purchased a crystal ball at Aunt Clarice's shop the previous Monday.

"Ah," said Dr. Moravec as she came in. "Clarence, I should introduce you. This is my granddaughter Ariel, who's living with me now. Ariel, Clarence Harshaw, a fellow of the Heydonian."

"Pleased to meet you," said Ariel, and came over to shake his hand. He glanced at her, blinked, and then for a moment the whites of his eyes showed all the way around. Then he mastered himself with a visible effort and said, "Likewise," and pressed her hand briefly. His hand felt cold and damp. "New—new in town, aren't you?"

"Yeah," said Ariel, putting on a smile.

"Well." He glanced back at Dr. Moravec. "Thank you again. Until next time." He forced some semblance of a smile onto his face, waited until the old man had replied, and then all but scurried out of the house.

"Well," said Dr. Moravec once he was gone. "That was—" He paused. "Interesting, I suppose, is the right word."

Ariel turned to face him. "Anything I can know about?"

"Yes, I think so." He went past her into the kitchen. She followed, stood in the doorway as he got the kettle on, nodded when his gesture inquired if she wanted a cup of tea.

"Harshaw's one of the Heydonian's shareholders," he said then. "He holds a little more than two percent of the total, and he's also one of the members of the committee that managed

Theophilus's shares. Apparently there are some serious irregularities about how the shares were handled, and some of the shares are missing. He wanted to inquire about the Board's position in all this. He also wanted to find out what I knew about a certain book titled *Liber Haatan*."

Ariel did a doubletake. "How did he know about that?"

"The note you took to Genevieve earlier today saw to that. I asked her to start making very public inquiries about the book, and to mention that I was interested in its whereabouts."

The kettle struck up a shrill whistle. Dr. Moravec filled the teapot, put it on a tray with two cups, and motioned toward the parlor. Once they were settled in their usual places, each with a cup of tea, he went on. "That was quite deliberate, of course. I mentioned this morning that I was waiting to see what kind of reaction that might get from the thief. Thus I was glad to hear from Harshaw. If he's already heard about it, so will nearly everyone associated with the Heydonian. Now we wait and see what happens."

Ariel gave him an uneasy look. "What might happen?"

He allowed a shrug. "Almost anything. The book might suddenly turn up. Someone might claim to have found it, or bought it, or been given it. The thief might contact me for some other ostensible reason. Or there might be magic involved, possibly of a dangerous kind. In any case, we should have more to go on shortly."

A silence came and went. Ariel considered him. She'd begun to learn how to read the faint clues that impassive face let by, and the traces she saw just then didn't comfort her at all. "You think there's going to be trouble," she said.

"That's quite possible." Another shrug dismissed the issue. "It struck me as a gamble worth taking—and there are very few kinds of trouble I can't cope with. If something happens you'll need to follow my instructions exactly, of course."

Ariel nodded and tried to convince herself she wasn't frightened.

CHAPTER 13

A NIGHT OF SORCERY

The trouble didn't take long to arrive. The first whisper of it came a little after dinner, while Ariel was washing up the dishes. What it was she could not have said at first: an odd sense of discomfort, maybe, as though something she could only just hear had her nerves on edge. She noticed it in passing, shrugged, and finished the dishes, thinking that it would go away soon.

It didn't go away. She went into the parlor and tried to settle down to read Lévi, but whatever it was that was bothering her would not let her go. A restless mood seized her, made the sofa feel awkward and uncomfortable. After ten minutes spent forcing herself to keep staring at the page, trying to get some meaning out of the words, she put the book aside and went upstairs to her room to find another book to read.

By the time she reached the room she was sure that something was dreadfully wrong. She could feel something she couldn't name filtering in through her bedroom window, whispering in the cold night air. It felt like fear and anguish and despair, like every bad day she'd ever had, but with the volume turned up as far as the dial would go. Worse, the room started to lurch and sway around her, and every sharp corner the furnishings had to offer seemed to jab at her, threatening. Panic surged. With it came a voice or something like one, screaming at her to run, to get away from whatever was gathering around her in the night. She fought down the panic, picked her way out of her room and down the hall toward the stair.

"Ariel?" It was her grandfather's voice, calling up from below.

She wanted to scream for help. Her hands clenched as she mastered herself. "Yeah," she called down. "Something— something's wrong. Really wrong."

"Yes. You still have the toby you got from Clarice Jackson, I hope. Can you locate it?"

If she'd been drowning and he'd tossed her a lifeline, she wouldn't have felt any greater relief, though a moment later she wanted to kick herself for forgetting so obvious a source of help. "I've got two of them," she said. "Yeah, I know where they are."

"Good. And use the bathroom before you come down. It may be a long night."

That got a shaken laugh from her, though she wasn't about to argue. She picked her way back into the bedroom, leaning on the wall most of the way—the entire house seemed to be making a slow sickening rotation around her. It took her two tries to open the desk drawer where she'd put both amulets, her hands were shaking that hard, but she managed it. The toby that had protected her from the witch of Criswell went around her neck first; the one she'd made a week before followed it a moment later.

The effect wasn't quite instant, but it was close. By the time the second toby settled into place the wrongness had started to fade, and in the moments that followed, it dropped away to a level she could manage. It did not go away entirely, though, and she could feel it rising again, pressing against the protection of the tobies. She closed the drawer with a steadier hand, used the bathroom, and then went to the stair.

He called up again as she reached the top step. "Do you need help getting down safely?"

"No, I'm okay." She started down the stair, and regretted her bravado at once. Each step seemed to twist and roll under her feet, as though it was trying to fling her down the stairwell headfirst. She nearly screamed for help then, but the thought of having to be carried down the stair by her grandfather was more than her pride could tolerate. A frantic grip on the stair rail steadied her, and she clambered down one step at a time.

Her grandfather was waiting for her at the stair's foot. "Sit down in the parlor," he said, "and do nothing at all. I mean that literally. It'll take me a few minutes to cast a protective circle, and I'm fairly sure the spell will get quite a bit worse."

"It's a spell?"

He nodded once. "Of a type I'm familiar with. I'll explain more once the circle's cast and we're both safely inside it."

Ariel went to the sofa and sat down. The thought of picking up a book occurred to her, despite her grandfather's warning, but the moment the idea moved through her mind, the sharp corners on the end table seemed to lunge toward her. She abandoned the idea, sat with her hands in her lap and her feet on the floor, and waited. Low sounds from her grandfather's study told of furniture being moved. Then, after a minute or so of silence, she heard his voice, murmuring syllables that didn't seem to belong to any language she knew.

Minutes passed. Finally he came out from the study and said, "It's ready. Get up slowly, and stay well away from the furniture once you start walking. You might bring a book to read if you like."

She got to her feet, felt the parlor begin to sway and twist around her, felt panic surge again and fought her way back to clarity. The only book within easy reach was Maude Gorton Wemberly's book on Captain Curdie's treasure. She bent to pick it up, saw the end table's corners poised to slash at her, moved her hand slowly to take the book and then straightened up. The room swayed again, but a few careful steps got her well away from the furnishings, and from there she picked her way carefully across the parlor to the study door.

Inside, her grandfather had pulled two armchairs into the center of the room and set them facing each other, and drawn a double circle in chalk on the hardwood floor around them, with strange words and symbols between the inner and outer circles. A gap on the side of the circle toward the door offered a way in. "Go in through the gap and take whichever chair you like," her grandfather said. He stood just inside the door with the chalk in his hand. "You'll probably have to sleep in it, so choose well."

The thought of trying to sleep was the last thing on Ariel's mind just then, but she went inside the circle and chose the chair that looked most comfortable. Once she was settled in it with Wemberly's book tucked beside her, Dr. Moravec came inside the circle, knelt down, and closed the gap with two lines of chalk and a few more letters and symbols, murmuring many-syllabled words under his breath as he did so.

The moment he finished, the pressure of the spell fell away as though a switch had been flipped. The panic and the disorientation weren't gone completely, but they lost so much of their force so quickly that Ariel sagged and let out a ragged breath in sheer relief. "Thanks," she said. "Seriously, thank you."

"You're most welcome." He stood up and then sat in the other chair, facing her.

"So what's happening? You said it was a spell."

"Yes. Someone's apparently decided to try to kill us both with magic. From certain aspects Mars is making with my birth chart just now, I was expecting an attack of some kind aimed at me, but not at both of us. I'm sorry—I would have warned you if I'd guessed."

"It's okay," she said.

A little shrug dismissed the remark. "I still should have given you more warning. Clearly I'll want to start keeping an eye on aspects to your birth chart, too. As for the spell, it's a classic malefic working, of a type that I've faced before. Quite clever in its own nasty way. Tell me this. When you were upstairs, before you put the tobies on, how did you feel? Frightened, perhaps, and unsteady on your feet?"

"Yeah. Like my whole life had gone wrong all of a sudden, the room was starting to spin, and everything was trying to hurt me."

"Exactly. The spell's intended to make its targets so terrified and confused that they start running. Once they do that, the spell will guide them straight into the path of a car, or down Lyon Avenue into Coopers Bay, or—" He shrugged. "Something else equally fatal."

Fear surged in her. She wrestled it into silence and said, "But you can stop it."

"Of course. Otherwise I wouldn't be alive today." He gestured at the circle. "There are various ways to keep a spell of that kind from having its effect. The methods I like to use are considered old-fashioned these days, but that simply means most mages don't really know how to cope with them. A spell as intense as this one can't be maintained for long, and the longer it's maintained, the more dangerous it becomes to the caster. So we wait."

"You don't do anything else," she ventured.

A quick shake of his head gave her the answer. "There's a clever trick that good martial artists know. When the other fighter tries to punch, instead of blocking it, they simply see to it that when the fist reaches its target, they're not in the way, and so it goes into empty air. If the other fighter isn't equally skillful, he loses his balance and down he goes."

That summoned an unwilling smile. "Daniel used to be really good at that."

"Was he? I'm glad to hear it. But that's the most effective strategy in dealing with a magical attack, and for a reason you need to know."

Ariel looked up suddenly, for her grandfather's voice had taken on a sudden edge.

"Malefic magic—magic that's done for an evil or destructive purpose—is much riskier than throwing a punch," he said. "It's particularly risky if the target knows how to get out of its way. In that case the energies summoned into the spell can't discharge themselves the way the caster intends them, and the only way left for them is to return the way they came."

She opened her mouth to ask what that amounted to, then realized the implication and drew in a sudden sharp breath. "Exactly," Dr. Moravec said. "The spell goes straight back to its sender and has its effect there. That's even more of a problem than you might expect, because casting a spell, any spell, attunes the caster to its energies. So defending against those energies is difficult work. Given what the spell was meant to do, it's not at all impossible that we'll see something in the paper in the next few days about a body turning up. What's the thing you say now and then? Play stupid games, win stupid prizes."

A long silence followed. The air in the study felt colder than the autumn night would explain. Ariel huddled down into the chair. What came to her mind then, absurdly, was the mustachioed villain of the Bertie Scrubb novels, Lord Roderick Dudgeon, whose inevitably foiled attempts to use magic to destroy the hero were reliable plot engines in that lucrative series. His spells were all standard Hollywood special effects—lightning bolts from the fingertips of his long black gauntlets, bat-winged otters with glowing green eyes materializing out of thin air, wicked weeping willows using their branches to grab at Bertie and his pals, and the like. Maybe it was just teenage cynicism, but she'd decided around the time of her fourteenth birthday that the couple who wrote the novels must have aimed at selling the movie rights all along.

Though she'd learned little enough about magic since coming to Adocentyn, she knew perfectly well already that magic couldn't do such things. What it could do—that was another matter, and not one she could answer in any detail yet.

The spell that surged out of the night at her that evening, and still hovered right outside the chalk circle, would have been hard to fit on a movie screen. The rising tide of panic and despair, the sense of vertigo that turned every sharp corner into a weapon lunging at her: how could a camera crew catch that? It was an unpleasant reminder that magic didn't have to make use of anything material to be deadly.

She shivered, found herself wishing that she had nothing worse to deal with than winged otters or Lord Dudgeon's sinister spying hedgehogs. Outside the chalk circle, shut out by her grandfather's magic but still present, the spell hovered in the darkness, edged with misery and dread. If she stepped outside the circle—

Panic flared in her again. She wrenched her mind away from the spell before it could get any more of a grip on her, and picked up the book on Captain Curdie's treasure. Dr. Moravec noted the movement and nodded once, acknowledging. She sent an unsteady smile his way. Then, with an effort, she turned all her attention to the beginning of the first chapter, in the hope of keeping herself from noticing the pressure from outside the circle.

It took some time, but eventually the book worked its own kind of magic and she lost track of everything but the story it had to tell. Somewhere, she thought, as Maude Gorton Wemberly set out everything known in her time about Bartholomew Curdie's last years, somewhere in Adocentyn, probably somewhere in this neighborhood, the old pirate hid whatever plundered treasures he'd kept from his voyages. Maybe there wasn't anything, but somebody thinks it's still there—

And maybe that person is willing to kill to keep anyone else from finding it.

That made her shiver, but she kept reading, and after a while the thought lost itself in the details of the British bombardment of Adocentyn during the War of 1812. Then she blinked awake, and only then realized that she'd fallen asleep. The book was still in her lap, but it had fallen half shut. If her grandfather had moved a single muscle since she'd dozed off she could not see any sign of it. Eyes open, hands resting on his thighs, he looked like a guardian statue in some ancient temple. The pressure of the spell outside the circle was still there, but it seemed distant, like a bad dream from some other part of her life. She closed the book, changed her position a little, and let herself sink back into a deeper sleep.

Time passed: how long, she did not try to guess. Now and then she surfaced just far enough to see her grandfather still keeping watch, and drifted back into sleep. The last time that happened, a first trace of gray light had started to filter in through the curtains. That cheered her, reminded her that the night would be over soon. She fell asleep again.

Then she was blinking awake suddenly, as though something had made a noise. Her grandfather was on his feet. Ariel sat up, blinked again and rubbed her eyes. A few moments passed before she realized what had changed: the spell had vanished.

"Awake?" Dr. Moravec asked.

"Yeah. More or less." Then: "It's gone, isn't it?"

He nodded. "It stopped not much more than a minute ago. It was already beginning to weaken, but this was very sudden. I'm sorry to say the chance of someone's body turning up soon is fairly high."

She processed that as he knelt, murmured unfamiliar words under his breath, and used a cloth to erase part of the chalk circle, opening a path to the door. No sudden rush of misery and terror followed. Ariel let out a breath she hadn't realized she'd been holding, and extracted herself from the chair. Her muscles yelled at her when she stretched, but she ignored them and followed her grandfather out of the study.

The parlor had the gray empty feeling of early morning all over it. Ariel took her book over to the end table and put it back in its place. The corners of the furniture showed no interest in lunging at her, which was some comfort. Dr. Moravec glanced around and then tilted his head, as though he was listening for some sound that he could hear and she couldn't. She watched him, wondered what he was sensing.

A moment passed, and then he turned to face her. "It might be sensible to get ready for the day without delaying too much."

Ariel nodded and headed upstairs without another word. She had just finished showering and was on the way back into her room when she heard the phone ring downstairs. A sudden cold certainty seized her. She dressed quickly and went back downstairs.

Dr. Moravec came out from the kitchen as she reached the foot of the stairs. "That was the police," he told her. "I'm sorry to say I was correct about the body. There's evidence of magic at the scene, so they've called me in."

"Okay," Ariel said after a frozen moment. "Should I come?"

"If you're willing."

"Of course I am."

"I'll need ten minutes or so," he said. "I don't recommend eating before we go, unless you're more used to corpses than I expect."

"Is—is it anyone I know, or someone I've heard about?"

A crisp nod answered her. "Clarence Harshaw." He went past her and climbed the stairs, leaving her to stare after him.

CHAPTER 14

A SHAPE ON THE SIDEWALK

The Buick rolled to a stop a few inches from the curb in a neighborhood north of downtown that Ariel didn't know at all. Big brick apartment buildings loomed up five and six stories into the gray morning sky, their windows mirroring the clouds overhead. Down at street level, landscapers had done their best with narrow strips of soil between sidewalk and brick wall. Their best wasn't especially good. People in fashionable outfits hurried in and out of the coffee shop at the end of the block behind the car. Elsewhere, nothing moved.

Ariel got out from behind the wheel, slung her investigations bag over one shoulder and followed Dr. Moravec along the sidewalk to the corner ahead. They rounded the corner to find a little clutch of people, some in police uniform, standing near two blue and white police cars and a big panel truck. The truck was painted in the same blue and white scheme as the cars, with ADOCENTYN POLICE—CRIME SCENE UNIT on the side. A short distance off, surrounded by yellow crime scene tape, a low limp shape lay sprawled on the sidewalk.

Ariel turned her gaze away sharply. She knew without having to ask that it was Harshaw, and she'd seen the dull red of drying blood around his head and the shards of broken window glass scattered all over the sidewalk, some of it marred with red stains of its own. A glance up didn't help, for

139

she could see the broken window, nearly as tall as a door, four stories above. Curtains fluttered in the breeze, half outside the gap. She knew at a glance that they must have been pulled outward by Harshaw's body when it fell.

One of the people near the police cars said something to Dr. Moravec, and he responded, but Ariel couldn't assemble the sounds into words. A bit of dialogue from the Somerset Maugham novel she'd read a few days back kept circling through her thoughts: "The dead look so terribly dead when they're dead." After a moment she realized she was being introduced to someone, and put out her hand automatically, but she couldn't focus her mind enough to absorb the name or appearance of the man whose hand she shook. The silent shape there on the gray sidewalk left her thoughts in tatters.

A woman in police uniform and a man in plainclothes turned and started toward the door of the apartment building. Dr. Moravec followed them, and after a blank moment Ariel realized that she should probably go with them too. She caught up before they'd gone through the door. The lobby inside had the bleak hollow feeling of a place no one ever used except to get to somewhere else. The elevator gaped open for them, slid gracelessly up to the fourth floor, spat them out into a corridor painted and carpeted in bland gray tones. Doors lined both sides of the corridor. One of them was open, and a uniformed policeman stood just inside it. He stepped out of the way. The policewoman stood back, and the other three filed in with Ariel last in line.

The sudden rush of cold air from the broken window jolted her out of the daze she'd been in since she'd spotted Harshaw's corpse. The curtains flapping in the breeze were the first things that caught her attention. Next she noticed the clutter of an interrupted magical working in the apartment's spacious living room. Four tall candlesticks stood in the four corners of the room, each one holding a candle of a different color.

Near the center, a small table covered with a black cloth had been knocked over. All over the carpet, flung down when the table went flying, lay an odd assortment of objects: an old book bound in cracked brown leather, a thin black wand ending in a claw that clutched a clear crystal sphere an inch across, a double-edged dagger with letters in a strange alphabet etched into the blade, and two ungainly shapes of wax that looked like they might have been clumsily made images of human beings.

She came further into the apartment, looked around carefully. The furniture looked expensive and fairly new. Two tall bookshelves were mostly full of antique books in good condition. A couple of attractively framed art prints hung on the walls. Doorways led into a kitchen and bedroom equally well furnished. A hint of incense hung in the air, though the breeze from the broken window had flushed most of it out.

Only when she'd turned her attention back to the living room did she spot a glint of reflected light just under the edge of the sofa. She crouched down to see it clearly, but the moment she'd noticed it, she knew what it was: the same sphere of yellow crystal she'd sold Harshaw at Aunt Clarice's shop.

The shock of recognition finished the job of clearing her mind. She considered saying something to her grandfather about the crystal, but he was in the middle of a conversation with the man in plainclothes: a police detective, she guessed, and one that her grandfather seemed to know well. He was a big man in every dimension, well over six feet tall, broad-shouldered and big around the waist. His dark brown skin contrasted with a camel-colored suit, a light pink shirt, and gold-rimmed glasses.

"The manager let them in, and this is what they saw," he was saying. "They snapped a couple of photos, put out the candles, called my department and got the hell back into the hallway. No sign of anyone else present, for whatever that's worth."

"There won't have been anyone else," said Dr. Moravec. "I'm familiar with this type of ritual. It's intended for one practitioner only."

"Well, that's something. Anything else I should know?"

Dr. Moravec went over to the incense burner, bent and sniffed. "At least two of the ingredients in the incense are psychoactive," he said. "It's hard to tell how much of each is in the blend, but it might be worth checking the victim's bloodstream."

The detective pulled out a tablet, typed something into it with quick deft thumbstrokes. "I'll let the medical examiner's people know."

"One other thing. I saw Harshaw yesterday. He came to my home to discuss Heydonian Institution business—we've got another tempest in our marble teapot, as you might have heard already. I can pass on as many of the details as you like, if they're of any use. The point that's relevant is that he seemed to be under a great deal of stress."

"Enough stress that suicide might be involved?"

Dr. Moravec glanced at him. "I have no idea. I didn't know him particularly well. Of course I'm not a psychologist."

"Got it," said the detective. "Just an idea." He started to turn away.

"Before you go," Dr. Moravec said then.

"Sure. What is it?"

The old man gestured at the brown book on the floor. "That matches the description of one involved in a case I'm looking into. If you don't mind my examining it—"

The detective motioned toward the book. Dr. Moravec pulled a pair of disposable blue gloves out of a pocket, slipped them onto his hands, went to the book and knelt beside it. Gingerly, touching the front cover only on its edges, he opened it. Ariel edged around the wreckage on the floor until she could see the pages inside. The first one was blank except for the brown spotting of aged paper, and so were the next three.

The one after that had a handwritten title in the ornate script of an earlier century. It took a long moment for Ariel to piece the curves and sharply angled lines together into the words she expected to see: *Liber Haatan.*

"The book you had in mind?" the detective asked.

"It certainly looks like it. I wonder if there's any way I could get access to it once your crime scene people are finished with them. I also wonder if any of your people noticed a crystal or a glass ball of some sort."

Ariel found her courage. "It's under the sofa," she said, and pointed. Dr. Moravec glanced at it and then at her, and nodded once, acknowledging.

"Good eyes," said the detective. "Part of the ritual, I imagine."

"I don't know," she said. "But Harshaw bought it at Aunt Clarice Jackson's shop on Moon Street on Monday. I was helping out behind the counter that day."

The detective considered her. "Cash transaction?"

"No, he put it on a credit card."

"Well, that's good. It'll be easy to trace." He turned to Dr. Moravec. "I'm not sure how soon Grady's people can get up here, but once they've taken some photos and checked for prints, yeah, you can sign them out."

"For investigative purposes only," Dr. Moravec said in a bland tone. The detective chuckled, shook his head, and left the apartment. Dr. Moravec and Ariel followed.

By the time they came out onto the sidewalk again, a van from the medical examiner's office had arrived and its crew was getting ready to take Harshaw's body off the sidewalk. Dr. Moravec started talking to one of the other police officers, but Ariel turned away from the conversation and the corpse. She kept her back toward that part of the sidewalk until she heard the van doors shut and the engine start up.

A moment after that happened, Dr. Moravec detached himself from the group and came over to where Ariel was standing. "Will your stomach tolerate coffee?"

She nodded, and he motioned with his head toward the corner. Once they were out of earshot of the police, he said, "You have very good eyes. I'm not at all sure I would have noticed the shewstone at all."

"If I was your height I wouldn't have seen it," Ariel admitted. "I don't think the detective spotted it either."

"Probably not. One way or another, that was very helpful." They turned the corner, headed for the coffee shop on the other end of the block. "Once I have the chance to read the book, it should be possible to answer most of the other questions I have about the case."

"The police'll just let you take it?"

"Temporarily. I've worked with the police often enough that they'll do me favors from time to time. Of course I'll have to sign for it, and if any of this business ends up in court I'll doubtless end up being called as an expert witness, but that's nothing new."

They walked the rest of the way to the coffee shop in silence. There was a short line inside. Once they had their coffee, Dr. Moravec said, "The car, I think." Ariel didn't argue. A minute or so later they climbed into the car and closed the doors.

"Harshaw was the one who cast the spell against us last night," Dr. Moravec said at once. "The incense he burns is standard for malefic workings of that general type. Also the wax figures—you saw them, I trust? Those were used to represent you and me."

Ariel sipped at her coffee. She'd gotten an Americano and put only a little cream and sugar in it; the clean harsh bitterness of it helped steady her. "I wonder why he went out the window," she said.

"That's simple enough. Think of the way the spell felt last night, and imagine the whole force of it affecting someone's mind all at once. He'll have been disoriented and overwhelmed with terror. He wouldn't have been able to think clearly at all, and once he tried to run, the spell will have made him mistake the window for a doorway. It wasn't safety glass, either—old plate glass, thin enough that a sudden blow was enough to shatter it."

Ariel shuddered, and said nothing.

"It's what he meant to do to both of us. By the way, there's no question why he aimed it at you as well as me. You saw him buy the shewstone at Clarice's shop."

"I sold it to him," Ariel said.

"Even more dangerous to him, once he discovered who you are. He must have been terrified that you'd told me about the shewstone: understandably so, if he stole the book, or bought it from the thief. The main questions that remain open at this point are what he was trying to do with the book and how exactly he got it."

"I thought he was looking for Captain Curdie's treasure."

"Very likely," said Dr. Moravec. "But we'll have to see what the book actually says."

Minutes passed, and then a low chime sounded: Dr. Moravec's cell phone. He pulled it out of a pocket, flipped it open, and said, "Yes?" The person on the other end of the call said something, and he replied: "Thank you. I'll be right there."

The phone went back into his pocket and he opened his door. "The police have finished with the book and the crystal. You may as well stay here."

Ariel nodded, and waited while he climbed out of the car, closed the door and headed back toward the scene of the death. He was back promptly enough with two mylar-coated plastic bags with zip closures. One glance at their shapes told Ariel what was in them.

"No fingerprints on either," Dr. Moravec said once he'd gotten back in the car. "The technician said that this kind of leather does a very poor job of taking prints, and the crystal must have been cleaned since it was last handled."

"Good," said Ariel. "Otherwise they'd have gotten my prints off it too."

"If they had, that would simply have confirmed your account." He reached around, got the bags settled on the floor behind his seat. "Now—what's the thing you like to say?"

Ariel managed a wan smile. "Let's ankle."

"A fine idea." She reached for the key, got the engine started.

Neither of them spoke on the way home. Once they were back inside the familiar house on Lyon Avenue, Ariel let out a long shuddering breath. "That was—kind of hard."

"It always is, the first few times," her grandfather said.

She glanced up at him. "You've probably seen a lot of corpses."

"A fair number. It's an occupational hazard in this business." He took the mylar bags to the door of his study, glanced back toward her. "First priority for me at this point is reading the book. For you—" A gesture indicated possibilities. "Whatever you need to do."

Ariel shrugged. "Deal, I suppose." He nodded, and went into his study.

An hour or so passed while Dr. Moravec read through *Liber Haatan* and Ariel sat huddled on the sofa, staring at nothing in particular and wishing the memory of Harshaw's body sprawled on the sidewalk didn't keep rising up so reliably in her mind's eye. Finally her grandfather came out of his study and sat in the usual armchair. She glanced up at him. He met her gaze and nodded, as though to say, yes, I know. The gesture comforted her a little.

"The book's not precisely what you guessed it was," he said then. "But it's close enough that the difference doesn't matter greatly. It's a grimoire, a manual of magic, and it includes spells to invoke thirty-six spirits. The first of them is Haatan, thus the book's name. Another, further back, is Thagrinus, the spirit of confusion, whose work was what we dealt with last night. All of the spells use a shewstone, though each has its own special requirements—that's standard in the old tomes. I've never seen another identical to this one, but there are twenty or so tolerably similar in the Heydonian's collections."

"I wonder why Harshaw didn't just use one of those," Ariel said.

"Oh, he had good reason. The older books in the collection can't be taken out of the building, and some of us know them well enough that if he'd made a copy and worked the rituals, we'd have known which book was involved." Ariel gave him a baffled look, and he went on: "No two magical rituals leave the same trace in the astral light. It's not that difficult for an experienced mage to tell when a familiar ritual's been worked."

She nodded and he went on. "So discovering an unknown grimoire that couldn't be traced back to the Heydonian, or to him, must have seemed like a godsend. How he found out about it—" Dr. Moravec shrugged. "I'll want to learn that if I can. But one way or another, he learned of it, stole it, and it seems fairly likely that he tried to find the Curdie treasure with it. That wouldn't have been a problem, except that the grimoire was stolen property and he'd be facing criminal charges if it came out that he had it. So when he guessed he was about to be exposed—" He shrugged again. "The spell that evokes Thagrinus must have seemed like the one way out. In a sense, I suppose it was."

Ariel waited a few moments and then said, "So do you think he found the treasure?"

"That's a question I can't answer. He had the book, the scrying crystal you sold him, and the other implements he needed, but the ritual also requires a scryer—someone who's able to see visions in the crystal. That's a little more complicated than usual, because the specific working to invoke Haatan requires that the scryer be a virgin."

That earned him a startled look. "Why?"

"Oh, that's a tolerably common requirement for scryers in some spells in the older sort of grimoires. You've read far enough in Lévi to find some of what he says about the astral light, I imagine." She nodded again. "The astral light is the life force. It's the power behind magic, but it's also the power behind sex. In a person who hasn't had sex, it's still—" He gestured. "Undetermined, I suppose, would be the best word. Afterwards, part of it is fixed in the reproductive centers. So there are certain magi-cal advantages to virginity. There are things a virgin, male or female, can do in magical workings that other people can't, and there are kinds of training that are best done while that's still the case. These days, that's not something that you find very often, for obvious reasons, but there it is."

Another moment passed. "Um," said Ariel.

Her grandfather glanced up at her.

"I am, you know."

His expression didn't change at all. "I didn't."

"Yeah. Nobody wants to boink the bookworm."

One of his eyebrows went up. "Then I'm not impressed with the young men you know."

She blushed. "Thank you."

"You're welcome." He considered her. "Are you saying that you're willing to try the ritual as a scryer?"

Ariel's throat went suddenly dry. She swallowed, managed to say, "Yes. Yes, I am." Then: "Well, if it's not going to be too dangerous or anything."

"Not at all." A quick shake of his head dismissed the idea. "All that's involved on the scryer's end of things is sitting in a comfortable chair and looking into a crystal for a time. One of two things will happen. Either you won't see anything in the crystal, and that's the end of it, or you'll see something, and we can proceed from there. I'll be present the whole time, of course."

She drew in a breath, and then closed her eyes. "Then—yes. I'm willing." She opened her eyes, looked at him. "Do you want to try to find the treasure?"

A nod answered her. "I'm convinced that that's the core of this entire business. I don't think we'll be able to unravel it until we know where Curdie left his treasure."

CHAPTER 15

A CHILD OF THE ELEMENTS

The ritual had to be done at noon or midnight. That was what the *Book of Haatan* said, and Ariel had already gathered that magical ceremonies didn't allow any wiggle room at all. By the time she'd made her offer, though, noon was too close to give Dr. Moravec enough time to make the necessary preparations. Ariel didn't mind. She could feel the strain of the night and its aftermath much too clearly. Once she was sure she wouldn't be needed for anything, she got some toast and coffee. When she'd finished those she went upstairs, washed up very approximately, and went to bed.

She didn't expect to sleep for more than an hour or two, but she blinked awake to find the flame-colored light of a gaudy sunset spilling through gaps in her curtains. She untangled herself from Nicodemus, ruffled his fur, made sure the bathroom was free, and then went through a second approximation of her morning routine.

The whole time, her thoughts circled around what her grandfather had said about virginity. The thought that the state in question might be any kind of advantage startled her, though second thoughts brought up dim memories of half-forgotten folktales in which only a virgin could do this or that. Those thoughts stirred other memories, too, most of them unpleasant. No one wants to boink the bookworm: that wasn't quite true, but none of the boys she liked were interested in her, and the ones who were interested too obviously weren't after anything but a surrounded cavity to use and then walk away.

The thought of still being a virgin on her wedding night had worried her now and then—what if she didn't know what to do, and bungled it? She'd known religious girls in school who meant to save themselves for their one and only, and she'd shaken her head and wondered what that sort of life was like. If virginity had advantages in magic, though, that put a different light on the matter. If she decided to go ahead with magical training, she added, and wondered why the idea didn't unsettle her as much as it had.

With all that repeating itself in her mind, choosing clothes took her longer than usual, but she settled on comfortable pants and a tee shirt and headed downstairs. The study door was shut but Dr. Moravec was sitting in the parlor with one of his old books open on his lap. "Good evening," he said as she entered the room. "I hope you'll be interested in pizza. I called in an order a while back. You'll need your stomach clear when the ritual starts but that doesn't mean you can't eat now—and we'll want leftovers after the ritual."

Ariel grinned. "Is that in the book?"

"No, but most of the lodges I've worked with had a habit of ordering pizza after serious ritual work."

"I could get used to that," Ariel said.

That got her a glance she couldn't interpret. After a moment: "The pizza should be here in thirty minutes or so. Other than that, have some tea if you like, and find something light to occupy your mind. The working will be more likely to succeed if we're both calm and relaxed."

"Okay," she said, and considered the books on the end table next to her. The two books on Captain Curdie and his treasure seemed too likely to send her thoughts in directions she didn't want to follow, so she picked up the volume of Dashiell

Hammett stories and opened it to the bookmark. "What are you reading?"

"Schopenhauer's *The World as Will and Representation*." When her face showed how little the title meant to her: "German philosophy."

She laughed. "Something light to occupy your mind."

One eyebrow expressed as much amusement as anything on his face ever did. "To each their own. Schopenhauer's been a favorite of mine since high school."

Ariel chuckled, and started reading.

The pizza showed up promptly, two extra large pies with sausage and double cheese, and two orders of bread sticks and marinara sauce to go with them. That and the adventures of Hammett's nameless detective, the Continental Op, kept Ariel pleasantly distracted until a little after eleven o'clock. That was when Dr. Moravec rose noiselessly and went into the study to make final preparations for the ceremony.

Once she'd watched him go and wondered what exactly he was doing, Ariel tried to turn her attention back to the next story in the volume, and failed completely. Uncertainties about the ritual ahead and cold memories of the night before put her nerves on edge. She realized after a little while that she'd read the same long paragraph at least four times and hadn't absorbed any of it. A fifth attempt didn't seem likely to have any better result, but she made the effort anyway. The grandfather clock with its strange dials seemed to slow a little further with each muffled click, and each faint noise that came out of the study made her jump. It helped just a little when she smelled incense, since that hinted that the ritual was actually going to happen soon, but more minutes passed after that, stretching out into what felt like a good-sized slice of forever.

Even so, when the door opened and her grandfather came out, Ariel let out a little frightened squeak. It wasn't just the suddenness of it, though she had no warning at all. It was the transformation in the old man. He'd put on a purple silk robe trimmed with gold, with symbols she didn't recognize embroidered all over it and a gold cord belt around the waist. A flat-topped purple cap sat atop his head, and something white was draped over one arm. The clothes weren't the only change. His face had a taut intensity to it she'd never seen in it before. It looked, in the yellow light from the parlor lamps, like an image carved of oak.

"Are you willing to proceed with this?" he asked.

Nervousness and the long wait nearly made her say something snappish in response, but she caught herself. The words weren't casual, she was sure of that. "Yes," she said. "Yes, I am."

"Then put this on over your clothes and come with me." He handed her the white thing on his arm. It turned out to be a white silk robe with a cord belt. She wondered at first if it was one of his, and would hang on her like a tent, but when she pulled it on over her head and got it settled she found that it fit her. That raised questions she didn't want to think about just then. She tied the belt and followed him into the study.

Four candles on tall candlesticks in the corners of the room provided the only light. By it she could see a double chalk circle traced around the center of the study, not quite like the one she remembered from the night before, with different words written between the lines. A small table stood at the center, with one of the two armchairs facing it. On the table glittered the yellow crystal ball they'd found in Harshaw's rooms that morning, the one she'd sold him at Aunt Clarice's shop just a few days before. Next to it was a fifth, unlit candle in a shorter candlestick, a spiral notebook, a pen, and the *Book of Haatan*.

A gap a foot or so wide broke both the chalk circles near the door. She gave her grandfather a questioning look, waited for his gesture, and went into the circle. He closed the door, followed her, turned, knelt, and finished the circle with chalk lines and a few more letters.

"Please sit in the chair," he told her, and went to stand on the side of the table furthest from her. "Don't leave it until I tell you it's safe." She nodded and settled into the armchair, then drew in a breath to ask him what else she needed to do.

The old man forestalled her. "Your part of this working is to wait until I tell you it's time, and then look into the crystal and tell me what you see. Don't look at it until I tell you it's time to do so. The invocation and the summoning will take maybe a quarter hour."

She nodded again, kept her gaze away from the crystal, and waited.

A few moments passed. Then through the door came the muffled sound of the grandfather clock in the parlor striking the first of twelve chimes, marking midnight. At that moment Dr. Moravec picked up the book, opened it, and began to recite something in a language Ariel didn't know. Latin? That was her first guess, but it had long words or names in it that didn't sound like Latin, or any other language she'd ever heard.

Nervous but fascinated, she watched her grandfather and noticed, very gradually, a change in the atmosphere. It wasn't like the change she'd felt the night before. There was no menace to it, and no disorientation. She simply felt the world stretching and shifting into an unfamiliar shape; unseen eyes turned toward her, somewhere out there in the darkness, but they weren't hostile. Curious? That felt a little less inaccurate, but only a little.

The eyes weren't human. That was the realization that came whispering through her mind a few moments later. Whatever they might be, the watchers weren't human beings, they had never been human beings, and their thoughts and moods were utterly alien to her. She drew in a ragged breath, kept waiting.

Her grandfather finished the recitation, paused, lit the candle on the table, and then began another recitation, subtly different. The sense of watchful presences got more intense. The words he was repeating seemed to blur into jumbled sounds in Ariel's ears, as though she was falling asleep, but she didn't feel sleepy at all. Her nervousness had fallen away. Her thoughts had gone silent. She waited, and presently she heard her grandfather's voice, as though from some great distance, telling her to look into the crystal.

Candle light sparkled in the golden stone. She stared at it, fascinated, and noticed without any sense of surprise that she didn't need to blink. Her attention rested on the brightness in the stone, and the rest of the world faded away around her.

More words she didn't know murmured in the distance. After a time—a few moments? A few hours? She couldn't tell—the glittering light in the heart of the crystal turned into something that looked like mist, and then swirled and cleared. Through it came a little figure. It looked at first like a child two or three years old, dressed in a short golden tunic and a little golden hat with a tall green feather in it, but the eyes that turned up toward hers were the eyes of an old man or woman, ancient and just a little amused.

She knew somehow that she didn't have to use words to speak to it. *Who are you? What are you?*

I am a child of the elements, the not-child replied. *And the one who summoned me knows my name.* Then, relenting: *I am Haatan. What would you have?*

The distant voice reminded her that she was supposed to say what she saw. In halting words, she described the not-child and repeated its words. The voice told her what to say in response. *The treasure of Captain Curdie*, she said. *It's somewhere in this town, not far from here. Will you tell me where it is?*

Has it not been claimed already? I told another its place.

She repeated that to the distant voice, attended to its reply. *If it's been found I haven't heard. If it's been moved, will you tell me where it's been taken?*

It has not been moved. Come with me. The glittering mist swirled, and suddenly she seemed to be standing on the side-walk on Lyon Avenue, with the house a dark shape close by and streetlights glaring orange against infinite darkness. The spirit gestured, and the two of them walked down the hill toward the harbor. The distant voice said something Ariel couldn't quite make out, but she recalled again that she was supposed to describe what she saw, and started naming each thing she noticed as she passed it. Her voice sounded far away, and Haatan didn't seem to notice it.

The night pressed close around the two of them, girl and spirit. No cars troubled the streets, no one else seemed to be walking anywhere in sight. Haatan stopped at one point and gestured up at a stone eagle—was it perched on the wall of a building, or hovering in the air? Ariel could not tell. They turned, or maybe the urban landscape pivoted around them, and they walked together down a street that seemed vaguely familiar to Ariel, though she could not remember why.

The distant voice told her to start counting the houses as she passed them. Numbers unraveled in her mind as she tried to think of them, and the best she could do was to say, "another house," and "another one," as she passed. Finally the spirit slowed, and pointed at something near ground level: a stoop of old gray stone, slightly hollowed on the top by the passage of feet across many years. Ariel described it as best she could.

The door above the stoop looked solid, but the spirit passed through it as though it wasn't there at all, and Ariel found that she could do the same thing. Inside, the house seemed to belong to a distant age. The entry was lit only by the coals of a fire glowing red in a hearth over to one side. Beyond it were rooms lit by yellow candlelight. Then another door that didn't have to be opened let onto a stairway that sank down into perfect darkness. Haatan gestured, and a pale light like a little floating flame came into being near them. It moved along with them as they descended the stair.

As they went down, something else caught Ariel's attention: the heavy dull sound of boots on the steps. She could see no one, but it sounded as though a group of men was hauling something heavy down the stair just ahead of them. For a moment she could almost see them, caught sight of dim yellowish flames surrounded by a haze of smoke, bent backs covered in coarsely woven woolen fabric, glint of metal. The image vanished nearly as soon as it came, though she described it aloud when the distant voice asked her to.

She and Haatan reached the bottom of the stair, and the pale light hovered close by. The spirit went around the foot of the stairs to the stone wall beneath it, tapped on the first of the big squared stones close to the ground: *tap*. It moved to the next stone, repeated the gesture: *tap*. It struck a third stone: *THUMP*.

The treasure is here, said Haatan. *The stone is thin, and behind is an open space. Do you understand?*

Yes, Ariel told it, and repeated the words to the distant voice.

Does this satisfy you, or do you desire more? The other desired more.

Startled, she considered the spirit. *Who is the other?*

A human. A shrug of the shoulders expressed the spirit's utter lack of interest. *It wanted more treasure. I found it enough to satisfy it, but it was a piece here, a piece there, for there are no other unguarded hoards in this little corner of the world of matter.*

Ariel repeated those words, too, and listened for the response from the distant voice. *I am satisfied,* she told Haatan. *Thank you.* Then, though the voice hadn't told her to say more: *I mean that. I'm grateful for your help.*

The old, old eyes regarded her. *You are gracious,* the spirit said. *I give you a gift in answer. When you come here in your body of flesh, you will see the ones who put the treasure here. That is how you will know that you have come to the right place.*

Thank you, Ariel said again.

All at once the cellar dissolved into shapeless glittering mist. Another moment, and Ariel blinked, squeezed her eyes shut, opened them again. She was still sitting in the armchair in her grandfather's study, wearing the white robe he'd given her.

The golden crystal was on the little table in front of her, and the candle beside it was an inch or so shorter than it had been.

Dr. Moravec hadn't moved. He waited for a few more moments, watching her, and then snuffed the candle on the table, turned a page in the *Book of Haatan*, and started to recite something else that sounded partly like Latin and partly like no language she'd ever heard before. As he spoke, the watchful presences in the night seemed to go somewhere else, and the world settled back to its usual shape.

Finally he stopped the recitation, closed the book, and set it down on the table. "It's finished," he said. "You can leave the chair now."

She got up, feeling unexpectedly stiff. "I hope I did okay."

"You did very well indeed." He took a cloth from a desk drawer, went to the side of the chalk circle near the door, knelt and erased enough of it to make an exit.

"I—I'm not sure how much I remember."

"Not to worry." Dr. Moravec stood. "I wrote down everything."

"Okay, good," said Ariel. "What should I do now?"

"If you'd like to get the kettle going, I'd be very grateful indeed." He motioned toward the study door. "The robe can go on the sofa for now, if you like. I should get all this cleaned up right away. Then? Pizza."

She nodded and went to the door.

Every little noise the old house made around her seemed unnaturally loud as she extracted herself from the robe, left it folded up on the sofa, and went to the kitchen to make tea. Dim sounds of traffic from outside, and the humming and occasional gurgling of the fridge set her nerves on edge. She was glad when the whistle of the kettle drowned out every other sound for a moment, and gladder still when her grandfather came out of the study, less exotically dressed and carrying the spiral notebook. He poured himself a cup of tea, sat at the kitchen table, and waved his hand at the pizza box, inviting her to have some.

She settled into her usual chair, picked up a slice of pizza, tried to figure out the best way to ask what she wanted to know. Before she found words, Dr. Moravec said, "A very productive working. We now know precisely where the treasure is." He took a slice of pizza from the box.

"You know," said Ariel. "I don't."

He bit into the pizza. Once he'd swallowed: "You went five and a half blocks toward the harbor, turned left, went along the south side of the street past twenty-six buildings, and then stopped at a very distinctive stone stoop in the colonial style. I recognized the stoop the moment you described it, and the number of buildings you passed confirmed the location. The treasure of Captain Curdie is hidden in the cellar of the house of a local contractor named Phil Benedetti."

Ariel looked up suddenly, eyes going wide.

Dr. Moravec regarded her. "That means something to you."

She opened her mouth, closed it again, swallowed, and said, "It means that Harshaw wasn't the one who stole the book. He had it, but he wasn't the only person involved. And—and it also means we're going to have to have a really difficult conversation with the Kozlowskis sometime soon."

After a moment, he nodded slowly. "Good. Yes, I'd begun to suspect the same thing. I can call them tomorrow after they're likely to be back from church, and then make another call or two." Then, motioning with what was left of his pizza slice: "Do have some. A full stomach will help close down your inner senses, and you'll need that if you want to sleep tonight. We can talk over the details as we eat. Tomorrow—" He allowed a shrug. "Tomorrow we'll need to be prepared for a different kind of trouble."

CHAPTER 16

AN HOUR OF RECKONING

"Thank you for being willing to talk to us on such short notice," said Dr. Moravec. Teresa Kozlowski, listening, nodded uneasily. Her brother made no response at all.

The parlor of the Kozlowski house hadn't changed noticeably since the day before, or for that matter since Ariel's first visit there. The same worn furniture braced itself against the burdens of another day. The children's toys in the corners had been rearranged a little, but it took a close look to spot the difference. Gray light came in through the windows from a bleak afternoon sky, though the rain still held off. Outside, just audible in the parlor, traffic moved up and down Holly Avenue: once again, no different from previous days.

The changes that mattered were in two of the people who sat there. Paul Chomski was once again wearing a bathrobe over slacks and sweatshirt, and sat half slumped on the sofa, but he looked as though his nerves were on edge. His eyes showed worry and anticipation, though he seemed to be trying his best to conceal both feelings beneath the usual tired smile. For her part, Teresa had a light in her face Ariel hadn't seen there before. She looked winded but happy, as though she'd put down a great burden. Ariel didn't have to wonder why. An elegant little diamond ring Ariel hadn't seen before sparkled on her left hand. Apparently Phil Benedetti hadn't delayed his proposal a moment longer than necessary.

"I have several things to pass on," Dr. Moravec continued. "The first is that the police have recovered the book that was stolen from you."

Watch their faces, he had instructed Ariel. Watch their faces and you'll know for certain. He was right, too, and she knew it the moments the words registered. Teresa's face lit up further with relief. It was Paul's face, as she expected, that turned suddenly pale.

"They won't be able to return it to you quite yet, however. Partly that's because it's evidence in an open case, of course, but there's another issue. It was found in the apartment of a man named Clarence Harshaw. The reason the police found it there is that they were called in yesterday morning to investigate Mr. Harshaw's death."

Teresa's hands flew to her mouth. "Oh dear God in heaven," she said. "Did he—did he do something with the book?"

"I'm sorry to say, yes, he did," said Dr. Moravec. "They found the book and certain ritual objects inside his apartment. He wasn't with them. He fell out a fourth floor window. They found him dead on the sidewalk."

A silence equally dead filled the parlor. Ariel kept her expression neutral and watched Paul. His gaze was fixed on Dr. Moravec. The tired smile he'd had earlier had tensed into a grimace. She braced herself for the part she was about to play.

"The police are still investigating," Dr. Moravec went on, "but they called me in as a consultant. That was how I learned about the book, of course. That wasn't the only thing they found at the scene, though. Some of the other things made this conversation necessary." He leaned back in the chair. "It turns out that your book wasn't the only thing that was stolen. There's at least one other item, of considerable value. But that also means that one or both of you haven't been entirely honest with the police, or with me."

That was the moment that mattered, and Ariel knew it. Blank looks and baffled responses could raise a barrier they might not be able to get past. Teresa gave Dr. Moravec the blank look, and opened her mouth to say something that almost certainly would work out to a baffled response. Before she could speak, though, Paul broke in, his voice low and hard. "Just what are you implying?"

That was Ariel's cue. "Mr. Chomski," she said, "do you remember the afternoon you told your sister about the plumbing problem? The day I helped her carry some yarn here from the Ivy Street Thrift Emporium? I happened to see something very odd while the two of you were looking at the pipes and the plaster. Joey was sitting on the floor over there with his stuffed bear Albert." She gestured. "And he was playing a strange little game. He was sitting there with the bear facing him, and the bear was looking down at something shiny—I think it was the plastic lens from an old flashlight. He had the bear staring at the lens."

That was too much for Paul. "You're lying!" he said, his voice rising.

"Paul." Teresa was staring at him. "No, she's not. I saw him doing the same thing a couple of times, and wondered what he was up to."

Paul opened his mouth to say something, thought better of it. Ariel went on. "I asked him what he was doing, and he said he'd promised somebody that he wouldn't tell. You know how kids when they're small, and they see something or do something they don't understand, something that troubles them, they'll act it out when they're playing? That's what Joey was doing. What he was acting out was one of the rituals in your family's book, and it's a ritual that has to include a boy or girl who's a virgin."

"That's a lie!" Paul shouted. "You're making that up!"

"Paul," Teresa said again, in an ashen voice. "You didn't."

"We can settle that very simply," said Dr. Moravec. "Ms. Kozlowski, maybe you'd like to have Joey join us now.

It won't be necessary to ask him to break his promise. All you have to do is ask him who made him promise not to talk. Once he answers—" He allowed a fractional shrug. "Then we can call the police."

Paul was on his feet in a moment, and his cane clattered to the floor. Ariel froze. Her grandfather had assured her, after consulting several horoscopes, that there was no risk that Paul would pull out a weapon, but she still braced herself for violence. Instead, Paul bolted for the entry. Teresa jumped up, too, and shouted after him, "Paul!"

For a moment Ariel wondered if Paul was going to go up the stairs, but instead he flung open the front door and ran out of it. Teresa went after him. By then Ariel was on her feet, too, and so was her grandfather. She sent an uncertain look his way. He started toward the door at a calmer pace, motioned with his head for Ariel to follow.

By the time she'd taken a step the sounds of a brief scuffle outside came through the open door. It ended as quickly as it began. Paul's voice, furious and shaken, shouted something, and another, deeper voice answered in the calm bored tones of someone repeating familiar words. She was in the entry before she could hear clearly enough to be sure the second voice was reading Paul his Miranda rights.

She reached the porch just behind her grandfather. There at the foot of the stairs stood Paul and two uniformed city policemen. They had him handcuffed and one of them, the officer she'd met at her first visit to the house, was just finishing up: "Do you understand these rights?"

Paul glared at him, but after a moment spat out, "Yes."

"Paul," said Teresa a third time. She was standing on the lowest step facing him, and her voice was taut with emotion. "Tell me why. I just want you to tell me why."

He gave her an angry glance and then looked away.

"I'm fairly sure I can explain," said Dr. Moravec. "The first of the spells in the book, the one he was trying to work with your son as the other participant, is meant to find hidden treasure. No doubt that sounds unlikely in this day and age, but this part of Adocentyn has at least one treasure hidden in it: Captain Curdie's."

Teresa turned around and stared up at him. "But—but that's just an old story." When the old man's expression didn't change: "Isn't it?"

"That's a question I can't answer yet. But that was what your brother was trying to do—he and his late partner Clarence Harshaw."

"That's another lie," Paul snarled. "I don't know this Harshaw person. I don't even know who he is. And this—this business about the Curdie treasure is ridiculous. Just to begin with, I can't even get out of the house most days. With my health problems, I'm not in any shape to go running around town looking for some imaginary treasure."

"If you're going to say that, Mr. Chomski," said Ariel, "maybe you should have been a little more careful about library books. Especially the ones you got from the fourth floor of the downtown library. You left bits of paper in a book on Captain Curdie's treasure, and the paper was torn off the top of a St. Adalbert Church bulletin."

Paul gave her a sudden horrified look, then forced his face back to a semblance of calm. "Anybody could have done that," he said. "Anybody who gets the bulletin, I mean, and there are 300 people in the congregation."

"Granted," said Dr. Moravec, "but you were the one who actually did it. We can settle that as soon as—ah, here he is."

An unmarked police car came up Holly Avenue and pulled over to park in a space just past the house. Out of it came the big detective Ariel remembered from the previous morning, dressed this time in a pearl-gray suit and a sky-blue shirt. He walked up to the officers, gave them and their prisoner an approving look, and said, "Nice. Been inside?"

"Not yet," said Officer Cabra. "This guy ran straight into us right here on the sidewalk. Can't complain about that, but we're still short of probable cause."

The detective nodded. "Fair enough. Grady's on his way."

"I think introductions might be in order," Dr. Moravec said then. "Ms. Kozlowski, this is Detective Lieutenant Leo Jackson of the city police. Lieutenant, Teresa Kozlowski. I don't think I have to introduce Mr. Chomski."

The detective gave him an amused look and turned to Teresa. "Ms. Kozlowski, I'm sorry to make even more of a mess of your Sunday, but your brother's a suspect in a couple of local burglaries. I can get a search warrant if I need to, but I always think it's polite to ask first, so I'd like your permission to search your house, and especially any rooms he occupies."

The last traces of calm in Paul's expression shattered. "No!" he shouted. "Tessie, don't let them in. You don't have to."

She rounded on him. "Don't you dare call me that. Do you hear me?"

His voice turned desperate. "That's my private space—"

"I don't care," she snapped. "I really don't. It's bad enough that you broke God's law and put your own soul at risk. But you had to bring poor Joey into it—" She mastered herself with an effort. "Tell me why, Paul. Right now. Tell me."

He glared at her, and then his gaze fell. "I wanted something for myself," he said in a low voice. "Just for once."

"Something for yourself," Teresa repeated. "Why, you little—" She caught herself again, struggled for calm. "You could have had plenty for yourself if you'd gone out and gotten a job instead of going on disability and begging me for a free place to live. I saw the way you jumped up and ran out here, without that cane of yours. I've wondered on and off for years if you were really as weak as you said. And now, this—" She shut her eyes, clenched her fists hard. "Officers, is there any way you can take him somewhere else? I really don't want to say the kind of things a Christian woman shouldn't say."

The detective nodded to the officers, and Officer Cabra said, "Sure thing, Ma'am."

"Give me a call when he's booked," said the detective.

"On it," said the other officer, and the two of them led a sullen and silent Paul away to their police car half a block further up the street.

Teresa turned to the detective. She was blinking back tears, but Ariel couldn't tell if they were tears of grief or of anger. "Yes, you have my permission to search the house, top to bottom. And the property too. Only—only first I should tell my children what's happening. They're six and ten, and I don't think they'd handle it very well if policemen just come inside and start going through everything."

"Mine are older than that," said the detective, "and I don't think they'd handle it too well either. Of course you can talk to your kids. In fact, if you're willing and there's someplace you can go, it might be a good idea to take them there. I promise you we won't make any more of a mess than we have to, and it might be easier for everybody."

"I—yes," said Teresa. "Yes, I think there's someplace like that. I—I'll need to call someone and ask, though."

"Of course," said the detective, and motioned toward the door. As she started up the steps he glanced at Dr. Moravec, who gave a crisp little nod and followed her at a distance. Ariel, not sure what was happening, went with him.

Inside, silence gripped the house. As she came to the stairs, Ariel looked up, and caught sight of Lucy and Joey crouched at the top landing, staring down with wide eyes. She sent a smile their way and hoped that it would help. Dr. Moravec stood in the parlor, and from the kitchen the sound of Teresa's voice came: "Phil? Yes, it's Teresa. The most horrible thing just happened. No, I'm fine and so are Lucy and Joey, but Paul's just been arrested for burglary." A pause. "No, I—I think he did it. But the police need to search the house, and—" Another pause. "Oh, thank you, thank you. Yes, please. That's what the detective said, too." Yet another pause. "Please. We'll be waiting out front. Phil, you're such a darling, I love you so much. See you soon."

The phone clattered back into its place. Dr. Moravec immediately turned and picked up the brown leather valise he'd left beside his chair, as though he'd just come in to retrieve it. He was straightening up with the valise in his hand when Teresa came back into the parlor.

"Dr. Moravec," she said, "can I ask you a question?"

"Of course."

"Do—do you think Joey's going to be okay?"

"Oh, he'll be fine. I recommend you talk to Father Novak, though, and you might consider arranging for a novena of St. Michael for his protection."

Teresa's face lit up. "That's a wonderful idea." Then, a little more tentatively: "You know quite a bit about Catholicism, I've noticed."

Dr. Moravec shrugged. "I grew up on the fringes of the Church, more or less."

"Well, you and Ariel would certainly be welcome at St. Adalbert's if you ever want to give it a try."

"I'll consider it," he said, and she beamed.

"Before you go," he went on, "this business isn't quite finished. Once you and Phil are comfortable with that, perhaps Ariel and I could pay a visit and pass on some other pieces of information the two of you need to know."

Her smile faltered. "Something bad?"

"No, quite the contrary." He extracted a business card and handed it to her. "Today, tomorrow, or whenever is convenient. I think you'll be very interested to hear about it."

She nodded uncertainly, said something indistinct, and then went to the stair and called up: "Lucy, Joey, we need to go visit Mr. Benedetti now. Lucy, can you make sure that Joey brings one of his stuffies? And bring a couple of books for yourself. Come right out front as soon as you can."

Light quick footfalls answered her. She went out onto the porch, and Dr. Moravec and Ariel followed her. The Crime Scene Unit van was just pulling up to the curb. Teresa went down to the sidewalk and stood there, saying nothing. For the moment, something like her old tired look settled back onto her face.

That changed a moment later when a big Ford four-door pulled up half a block away and Phil Benedetti flung himself out of it. By then the plainclothes officers from the Crime Scene Unit van were conferring with Lieutenant Jackson, and Lucy and Joey had just come out onto the porch, Lucy with two books in her hand and Joey clutching Albert Bear, but as far as Ariel could tell the builder noticed precisely one person in the world just then. He came pelting up the sidewalk at not much short of a run, took Teresa's hands in his, and said, "You're okay? Just tell me that you're okay."

For answer Teresa started crying, and Phil gathered her up in his arms and held her for a little while. She said something to him in a quiet voice, kissed him, and then went to gather up her children while Phil walked over to the detective. A few moments and not many more words later, Phil bundled Teresa and the children into his car and drove off. As soon as they were gone the officers of the Crime Scene Unit hefted cameras and rucksacks and headed into the house. Dr. Moravec went to talk to the detective. Ariel followed, because a certain detail had just fallen into place and she wanted to confirm it.

"Nice job," said Lieutenant Jackson. "We'll see what Grady's people find, but I'm pretty sure he's the one we've been looking for. The only question is what happened to the goods."

"If I had to guess, they're in his room, or somewhere in the house," Dr. Moravec said. "You'll remember the thing he said: 'I just wanted something for myself.' Some people steal for the money, but for some, it's not that, it's the mere longing to have things."

"Here's hoping. Well, I'll keep you posted."

Dr. Moravec thanked him and started to turn to go. Before he could get far, Ariel said, "Lieutenant Jackson, I don't want to pry or anything, but do you have a daughter named Cassiopeia?"

The detective grinned. "I didn't think you registered that yesterday. Yeah, I'm Cassie's dad. She's been talking about you practically nonstop for a couple of weeks now, you know."

Ariel blushed, then grinned also and said, "Should I tell her you said that?"

"Sure. It won't slow her down for a minute." One of the plainclothes officers came out onto the porch, and Lieutenant Jackson glanced that way and said, "Dr. Moravec, Ms. Moravec, duty calls. See you later."

He went up to the porch. Ariel and her grandfather walked to the big black Buick, and climbed in. Once she'd fastened the seatbelt, she half turned to face him. "What are you going to tell Teresa and Phil? If you say anything about Haatan I don't think they'll handle that well."

"Not at all," he agreed. "In this business it's sometimes necessary to frame things in terms that people can understand. We'll say there was something written in Harshaw's apartment."

"Okay." She turned the key, started the engine. "Are you really going to think about going to St. Adalbert's?"

A quick precise shake of his head answered her. "No, I was simply being polite. I left that kind of religion behind by the time I was your age." He tilted his head, considering her. "If you'd like to go yourself, of course—"

"Nope." After a moment: "I think there's a God, but that doesn't feel like the right way to deal with Him. Well, for me, at least. It seems to work pretty well for Teresa and Phil."

Dr. Moravec nodded. Ariel eased down on the gas pedal and pulled away from the curb.

CHAPTER 17

A QUEST COMPLETED

The familiar quiet of the house on Lyon Avenue wrapped around Ariel like a comfortable blanket once she shed her jacket and went into the parlor. Low noises, not loud enough to break the hush, spoke of Dr. Moravec going into the kitchen, getting the kettle on the stove for tea, and then checking for messages on the phone. As Ariel sat down on the sofa, feeling tired and a little lost, she heard the kettle start to mutter to itself. Moments passed, and then Dr. Moravec's voice sounded. "Good afternoon, Theophilus. Your message sounded almost perturbed."

Ariel looked up sharply, waited through the long silence that followed. "Are you asking me in my official capacity?" Another silence, shorter, came and went. "That seems sensible to me. I don't imagine that you'll have any trouble recovering them." Another long silence, then: "That's good to hear. Please keep me posted. Anything else? Until later, then."

The phone settled back into its place as the kettle cleared its throat and started to sing. Not long thereafter Dr. Moravec came into the parlor, handed her a cup of tea, and took another to his armchair, where he sat.

"That was Theophilus, as you probably heard," he said.

"What does he sound like when he's perturbed?"

That earned her a raised eyebrow. "Calm, quiet, and very precise," said Dr. Moravec. "The quieter he gets, the more trouble someone is going to be facing. He was very quiet indeed when he left his message."

She glanced up at him from her tea, nodded.

"But he provided another piece or two of the puzzle we've been assembling. Quite a few of his stock certificates were extracted from the safe-deposit box where they were kept, as I thought. They've been located, I'm glad to say, and there's no question who took them: Clarence Harshaw. He had access to them, as the chairman of the committee, and it turns out he used them as collateral for loans from one of the less honest local banks. The bank's in serious legal trouble now, since their people must have known that Harshaw had no right to the certificates, but at least they've returned them to Theophilus. So that much is taken care of."

"Loans," Ariel asked. "How much?"

"Well over 200,000 dollars. You saw Harshaw's apartment. That's not a cheap neighborhood to live in, and he had new furniture and certain other expensive habits. He must have been living well beyond his means. No doubt he assumed, as so many of us did, that Theophilus would never come back, and his game with the stock certificates would never be uncovered. Once Theophilus returned, of course, Harshaw would have had to find a great deal of money in a hurry so he could reclaim the certificates and get them back where they belonged. Or he'd have to sell his own shares to cover the debts, and lose all his rights as a shareholder."

Ariel nodded slowly. "That'll explain why he looked so scared when he bought the shewstone at Aunt Clarice's."

"And when he came to speak to me as well. He was always a nervous type, but not to anything like that degree."

Ariel nodded again, and sipped her tea. As she was setting the cup back down, the phone rang. She flung herself to her feet, went into the kitchen and answered it. After a little while, she stuck her head back into the parlor and said,

"It's Teresa Kozlowski. She says she and Phil are ready to talk to us." With an uncertain smile: "She says they both want to get it over with, whatever it is."

Dr. Moravec finished his tea and got to his feet. "Excellent. Are you up to walking there? It might be educational to follow the route you were shown by Haatan."

"Sure," said Ariel. "I'll let her know we're on our way." She ducked back in the kitchen.

Late afternoon spread itself above Adocentyn a few minutes later as the two of them came down the steps to the sidewalk and turned south, toward the harbor. A brisk wind had picked up, making Ariel glad for her jacket. Dr. Moravec's long black woolen coat flapped around him like a wizard's cloak. Neither of them spoke. Ariel tried to remember as much as she could of the route she'd been shown by the spirit. What was going on behind her grandfather's impassive face was as usual a complete mystery to her.

As they reached the corner of Gold Street, she stopped cold as vision and reality finally came into contact. "There was an eagle in the air right there. It didn't look quite like that one, but close." Her gesture indicated an old brick and stone building, once a bank, now a coffee shop. Above the doors, carved into the stone in a century-old patriotic gesture, an eagle had its wings spread and its beak open in a silent cry.

Dr. Moravec nodded, and they turned onto the sidewalk. Gold Street dipped, and then rose up again to a low knoll that must once have had a fine view of the harbor and the tall ships anchored there. Ariel tried to remember how many houses she'd passed in the vision, gave up after the memory twisted and blurred, and let herself be drawn along the final steps of the quest for the old pirate's treasure.

One block after another passed, and finally they passed the sign announcing Phil Benedetti's business and came to his front door. The door was raised a little above street level, and the single step leading up to it was a gray fine-grained stone. Ariel gave it a close look, and noticed two things. The first was that it wasn't a kind of stone she'd seen anywhere else in that part of town. The second was that it was dished in the center, as though worn down by many years of use.

While Ariel was still processing that, Dr. Moravec went up to the door and knocked. A few moments passed and then Lucy Kozlowski opened it. "Hi," she said, and then looking past the old man: "Oh, hi, Ariel." To both of them: "Mom and Mr. Benedetti are waiting." Dr. Moravec motioned to her to lead the way.

The entry was bigger than Ariel expected, with what was pretty obviously a sealed-up fireplace on one side: a colonial builder's habit, a scrap of memory whispered. Beyond that was the parlor, a pleasant though mostly undecorated room with white plaster walls and old but sturdy furniture. Teresa and Phil were sitting together on a big brown sofa. He was beaming, while she had red eyes but a luminous expression on her face, and her lipstick was smudged. Over to one side of the room, uninterested in the others, Joey sat on the floor with Albert Bear, talking to him in a quiet voice.

"Teresa tells me you have something to pass onto us," said Phil, once Dr. Moravec and Ariel had been waved to chairs. "I'm all ears."

"It's quite simple," said Dr. Moravec. "I imagine that Ms. Kozlowski told you what her brother seems to have been doing, along with an accomplice." Phil nodded. "You probably also know that the accomplice fell out of a fourth story window yesterday morning. The police found certain notes in his apartment, and I read those when I was called in to help with the investigation. If the notes are correct, Captain Curdie's treasure might just possibly be hidden inside one of the walls of your basement."

Phil's mouth fell open, and for a minute or so he tried to speak without much effect. Teresa opened her mouth, too, and then shut it. Lucy, who had gone over to sit near Joey, stared with round eyes. Finally Phil forced out, "You've got to be kidding me."

"That's what the notes said." Dr. Moravec shrugged.

"In my basement? Seriously?"

"The foundations of this house are from the colonial period, I think."

"Yeah, but—" He stopped. "Yeah," he said more slowly. "Probably before 1750 was what I got told before I bought the place."

"The notes gave a specific location in the basement, too. The stones there are supposed to be only a few inches thick, with an empty space behind them. Is that accurate? I know of only one way to settle the question."

Phil processed that. Teresa drew in an unsteady breath and said, "Do you have any idea where Harshaw got that?"

"None at all. He might have found something in the Heydonian Institution archives, for all I know. All we have is a description."

She nodded uneasily. Phil, having clearly come to a decision, hauled himself to his feet. "Well, we won't figure anything out by sitting here. Let's go see."

"Should I stay here with the children?" Teresa asked him. Lucy sent a look half pleading and half outraged toward her, but Phil shook his head hard. "Not a chance," he said. "If there really is some pirate treasure down in the basement, they're gonna want to see it. Wouldn't you, when you were their age?"

A little procession of four adults, two children, and one bright blue stuffed bear duly trooped back to the kitchen, and from there to a door in an unobtrusive corner. Phil opened it, revealing a stair downwards. Dr. Moravec motioned to Ariel, and she made herself smile and nod and go to the stair.

The moment she started down it, it felt as though she was back in her grandfather's study staring into the shewstone, following Haatan along a stair into darkness. There wasn't much darkness on the stair in reality, big bright bulbs in ceiling fixtures saw to that, but every step made that harder for her to notice. The stair felt dark, midnight-dark, and the only light that guided her was—

Flame. She could see two red smoky fires, neither of them large or bright, one close by her, the other further down the stair. They smelled of hot grease and cast a dim flickering light on the gray stone that lined the walls and ceiling. Her eyes protested that the walls and ceiling of the stairway were covered with smooth white plaster, but her mind couldn't process what they were saying. Moments passed and she could see the flames a little more clearly. They rose from old-fashioned rushlights held by calloused, muscular hands.

She kept going. The ones who held the rushlights were burly men, tough and scarred, in the knee breeches, waistcoats, loose shirts, and buckled shoes of colonial times. More men of the same kind came behind. Ahead, a single figure led the way, older than the others and more ornately dressed. She could almost hear their footfalls on the stone steps. The men behind her carried something heavy, she knew that, and the weight wasn't wholly physical. People had died because of that burden. The footfalls stretched and blurred into other sounds, far off but recognizable: roar of cannon, clash of steel, voices raised in fury or terror, until a sudden hard sound like the lid of a chest being slammed shut cut them off.

The men kept going, and so did Ariel. Finally they reached the foot of the stair and went on into the dim cluttered spaces of the cellar. Back behind the stair, a few stones in the cellar wall at floor level had been pulled out, revealing an open space a few feet high and wide and deep, just the place to hide the thing they brought. She stepped aside as the men brought their burden down the last steps, and the man who led them turned to face her.

She recognized the face at once from the illustrations in the books she'd read: heavy brows, hooked nose, jowls big and loose with good living. She recognized the periwig, too, the neatly pressed curls framing the face and spilling down over the shoulders. The famous Captain Curdie was a plain-faced, middle-aged man, tall and heavily built, wearing an ornate great-coat, knee breeches and buckled shoes, with lace gathered fussily at his throat. For a moment his eyes seemed to focus on Ariel, and he allowed a wry smile and said seven words she couldn't hear, but could almost make out from the motions of his lips.

Then all at once Ariel was standing in a well-lit cellar with old stone walls, light fixtures on the ceiling, and power tools close by, surrounded by people who couldn't have looked less like eighteenth-century pirates if they'd worked at it all day.

The change didn't disorient her enough to matter. "Right here," she said, walking over to where the hole in the wall in the wall had been. "It should be right around here."

Phil gave her a quizzical look. "Okay, let's give it a try." He went to the tool rack on the other side of the basement and returned with a hammer and a piece of board. Over to one side of the hole she'd seen, he put the board against the stone and tapped with the hammer, hard: *tap-tap*. Phil moved board and hammer six inches or so, tried again: *tap-tap*. Another move brought it closer: *tap-tap*.

One more move: *THUMP-THUMP*.

That got sudden startled looks from everyone in the cellar but Dr. Moravec. Phil shifted the board back a short distance, tapped again, figured out where the deep hollow sound began, then kept going, looking for the place where it ended. The hollow sound came from behind two stones, just large enough to hide the gap Ariel had seen.

"Well," Phil said then. "Who'd have thought."

"Can you open it up?" Dr. Moravec asked him.

"Piece of cake." He went to the other side of the cellar, came back with a chisel and a different hammer. Mortar sprayed out as he put them to work. After a few blows the sound of the chisel shifted abruptly. Phil pulled it out and said, "There's space behind it, all right, and the mortar's only about an inch deep. Wow."

"If you need any help—" said Dr. Moravec.

"Nah, I got it." He went back to work with the hammer and chisel.

Two minutes later the first stone was loose. Phil pushed and pried, got it to slide out, hauled it from its place and dragged it over to one side. Darkness hovered behind it. It took another minute or so to get the other stone loose, and then everyone, even Dr. Moravec, craned to look. The space behind the stones went back into shadow, and a dark rectangular shape that looked like an old trunk or chest filled most of it.

"It's probably fragile," Dr. Moravec said then, "and quite heavy."

"Gotcha," said Phil. He went to the other side of the cellar again. While he was gone, Joey made a spirited attempt to get to the gap, and had to be corralled by his mother and Lucy.

"Here we go." Phil came back with the sort of canvas strap Ariel had seen holding down loads on a pickup. It took a little work for him to slide it through the gap over the top of the chest and get it settled around the back. Once the strap was in place, he got a solid grip on it, and leaned hard. Inch by inch, the shape slid grudgingly out into the light and onto the floor of the cellar: a sturdy wooden chest with an arched top, bound together with rusted metal, and held shut with a lock that looked centuries old.

The hasp succumbed promptly to a crowbar. Phil tried to heave the lid open, got nowhere, applied the crowbar. The hinges groaned and then snapped, and the lid went up.

"Holy Mother of God," Phil said in a toneless voice.

"I think I need to sit down," said Teresa, sounding faint. Dr. Moravec went over to her and helped her sit on the steps.

Ariel scarcely noticed. She stood there staring, trying to process the gleam of aged gold and the glint of jewels, red, green, blue, and white, that filled the chest.

It was Lucy who said aloud what all the others were thinking. "That's real, isn't it?"

"Yes, I think so," said Dr. Moravec. To Phil: "May I?"

"Sure thing," Phil said. He still sounded stunned.

Dr. Moravec went to the chest, pulled out a coin that glinted yellow in the light. "You'll have to get a professional to assess the rest of it, but this is certainly gold. A doubloon, I think. This—" He put the coin back, extracted a stone that blazed red. "A very fine ruby. I wonder what this is." He pushed aside more coins, pulled something out from among them: a golden statue a foot high, of a Hindu god with an elephant's head. "A statue of Ganesha. Curdie must have brought that back from one of the Mughal treasure fleets he raided."

"Mom," said Lucy, "can I touch some of it? Please?"

"Well, I don't know," Teresa said. "There might be something sharp—"

"Let me take care of that," said Phil. With a motion of his head: "Lucy, Joey, why don't you come over here." Both children trotted over. "Cup your hands like this." Once they'd both done it, Phil scooped out a handful of coins and put some in each of their hands. "There you go. That's real live pirate treasure you're holding."

Round eyes answered him. "What do you say?" Teresa prompted, and they stumbled through thanks, staring at the impossible. For her part, Ariel stared just as blankly, trying to shake off the conviction that she must be dreaming.

Phil shook his head, turned to Dr. Moravec: "I don't know what I'm supposed to do about something like this. I mean, who even owns this stuff?"

"You do," said the old man. "Under state law, when you bought the property, you bought anything in, around, and under it. About twenty years ago I was involved in a case a little like this, a matter of certain rare books that had been hidden inside a wall. The owner of the house made quite a bit of money selling those to the Heydonian."

Phil blinked, and then slowly began to nod. After a moment he walked over to Teresa, gave her a hand up, and said,

"You know what I think? I think the Lord brought us together and then He decided to give us a really special wedding present."

She shyly put her arms around him. Ariel looked away as they kissed, feeling vaguely embarrassed. Lucy glanced up from the pirate treasure in her hands, saw them, and giggled.

After an interval, Phil came back over to where Dr. Moravec was standing. "Okay," he said, "one more question. Any chance you know how to go about dealing with this kind of thing? You said a professional ought to go over it, and that sounds like a really good idea to me, but I don't have a clue how to go about finding one."

"It's not too complicated," said Dr. Moravec. "The state police need to be informed, and they can put you in touch with the state historical preservation office. That's the office that will help you get it properly assessed, and of course put someplace secure. I can call the state police if you like—I know some people at their Adocentyn office."

"Could you, please? That'd be a big help." He managed a shaken laugh. "I'm still trying to get myself to believe that it's real."

"I'll be happy to." Dr. Moravec went to the stair and glanced at Ariel, who caught the implication and followed him up out of the basement.

"I saw the pirates," she said in a low voice once they were in the parlor upstairs. "When I started down the stairs, it was like I was with them. And—"

All at once she started laughing. "And I know what the words are that Curdie told his servant to carve on his tomb. He said them to me, when I was watching, and I couldn't hear him but I could read his lips, almost. 'Strike ye stones below in ye cellar.' That was the secret."

Dr. Moravec considered that, and one of his eyebrows rose. He nodded, then got out his cell phone and started tapping the screen.

CHAPTER 18

A CHOICE OF MAGICS

"If you ever let on that you're jealous of me again," said Cassie, "I'm going to laugh right in your face. I mean it." She was grinning as she said it.

"Come on. I only gave my grandfather a little help on a case."

"Only. Like everybody does that all the time. Let me spell it out for you: P, I, R, A, T, E, T, R—" Ariel started laughing, and so did she.

Monday had arrived, and they sat in the back room of the shop again while rain drummed on the windows behind them. The day's work involved garbling another brown paper grocery bag's worth of plant matter: long thin brown roots, twisted and mixed with dirt. They were from a tree called crampbark, but the roots had the fine colorful name of devil's shoelaces; they looked like it, too, and the process of getting them untangled and free of dirt wasn't quick or easy. Ariel didn't mind. They were powerful protective herbs, Aunt Clarice had explained. If you knew how to do it, and tied a knot in one of them, it was like tying the devil's shoelaces together so that he'd trip over his own cloven feet.

"Well, you didn't tell me," Ariel said then, still laughing, "that your dad's a police detective, in charge of—what did you call it? Department S?"

"Yeah," Cassie admitted. "S for spooky. Every big police department has somebody who handles cases like that. It's normal."

"He probably does as much magic as my grandfather," said Ariel.

Cassie shook her head. "No way. He doesn't do magic at all." Faced with Ariel's disbelieving look, she temporized. "Well, okay, he uses tobies for protection sometimes and some other things, but everybody does that."

Ariel just kept looking at her, and after a moment she capitulated. "Okay, everyone in my family. And a lot of other people in Adocentyn, too. Your grandfather's still one of the most famous mages in town, you know. Has he taught you anything yet?"

"No, not really."

"Maybe you should ask him. I don't mean hint at it, girl. Sit him down and ask him. Sometimes you have to do that, you know."

Aunt Clarice came into the room to check on them then. After she left, their conversation veered in other directions. Over the days that followed, though, Ariel thought about Cassie's words much more than once.

That Monday, and for the two days that followed, it didn't seem as though she would have the chance to ask her grandfather anything at all. On each of those days, Dr. Moravec left early and came home late at night, meeting with the Board of Trustees, meeting with the remaining members of the committee that had managed Theophilus Cray's shares in the building, meeting with various other groups and individuals about which she knew less than nothing. She guessed, from stories about the Heydonian he'd passed on earlier, that the negotiations were all conducted with the elaborate courtesies of an earlier era, but there were serious issues involved, and Dr. Moravec came home all three nights looking tired and strained.

Ariel knew better than to bother him. She concentrated on her studies with Aunt Clarice and on the last dozen or so chapters of Eliphas Lévi's book, and read the newspaper stories each morning as they chattered enthusiastically about Captain Curdie's treasure. The chest and its contents had been hauled away by an armored car Sunday night to the vault of a local bank. Nobody was sure yet exactly how much it was worth but the newspaper waved around estimates in the high six figures, maybe as much as a million dollars. Phil and Teresa had already told the paper that ten percent of the value was going to their church, and the paper had interviewed Father Novak, who sounded flustered and pleased even through the sedate medium of newsprint.

Ariel didn't mind those three solitary days, because she had serious thinking to do. When she'd come to Adocentyn, magic had been something she'd assigned regretfully to the category of make-believe and wishful thinking. Her experiences in Criswell had taught her otherwise, but left her with very little sense of what magic was and how it worked. Now she had a clearer sense, and knew that a choice waited for her. She could back away from magic altogether, the way so many people did. She could keep on dabbling in it, making a few tobies or casting other simple spells, the way many other people did. Or—

That last thought always brought to mind the dark slumped shape of Clarence Harshaw's corpse on the sidewalk, and then her grandfather's words about the perils of evil magic. Not all magic was evil, though; she knew that now, knew it in her bones. The protective circle and the tobies that kept Harshaw's working from killing her, those weren't evil, and her encounter with Haatan had been a strange experience but there was no evil in it. There were spells to stop evil magic and other spells to bring blessing and healing. That she knew. The question was purely whether she would be one of the people who cast them, and she brooded over that on all three nights, staring out the window of her bedroom at the lights of the city.

Thursday was another busy day for tea leaf readings, or so Aunt Clarice had said Wednesday afternoon, and so Ariel had the day to herself. Dr. Moravec went out before she got out of bed, leaving a note that simply said *No idea when I'll be back. Plan accordingly.* She made toast and coffee, washed the morning's dishes, and then brought in the paper and spread it out on the kitchen table as usual.

The story about the Curdie treasure had mostly fallen off the front page, though an article toward the bottom talked about a speech by a diplomat from the Indian consulate: Phil and Teresa had donated the statue of Ganesha to the Indian government as a stolen art treasure, and the diplomat was there to thank them for it. In the local section, facing the police blotter page, a terse story announced that Paul Chomski, 34, resident of Adocentyn, had been arraigned on seven counts of grand larceny. Ariel shook her head and kept reading.

She was most of the way through her task when she heard the rattle of the mailbox out front and went to check. Most of the day's mail was nothing out of the ordinary, but one small elegant card in a square envelope caught her attention. It had Teresa Kozlowski's name on the upper left corner, and it was addressed to Ariel as well as her grandfather, so she opened it once she'd brought the mail back indoors. It proved to be a wedding invitation from Teresa and Phil. No surprises there, she thought, and put it with the rest of the mail on the coffee table.

Once she'd finished clipping stories and put the results on her grandfather's desk, she made herself another cup of coffee and sat down to tackle the last chapters of *Dogme et Rituel de la Haute Magie*. The French came more easily to her now that she had a couple of weeks of practice. Hours passed, the coffee vanished a sip at a time and got refilled, and a little after two in the afternoon she finally reached the appendix with the list of spirits. Haatan's name was still in its place, and she wondered if she'd ever encounter that strange being again.

She got up to refill her coffee mug again before tackling the last pages. Just then the front door rattled and opened, and Dr. Moravec came in. Startled, Ariel went into the kitchen anyway and got the kettle heating for tea instead, then went back to her corner of the sofa.

The old man nodded a greeting, and put a yellow plastic bag marked EVIDENCE on the coffee table not far from the mail; it had something in it that looked like a small cardboard box. He settled into his armchair, closed his eyes for a moment, opened them, and then said, "Thank you for getting tea started. This whole process turned out less difficult than I expected, but—" He let the sentence trickle away.

"The business with Mr. Cray's shares?"

"Yes. It could have ended up in the courts. Fortunately we avoided that, and this morning we reached a settlement that no one likes but everyone can accept. So I had time to go to the Public Safety Building to meet Leo Jackson and get handed a slightly different perplexity. What do you think about Teresa Kozlowski and Phil Benedetti? Are they well suited to each other?"

Startled by the sudden change of subject, Ariel blinked, but said, "Yeah. Yeah, I think they'll be really happy together."

Just then the kettle started singing, and she got up, fixed tea, and brought out a teapot and two cups. "Thank you," Dr. Moravec said once she'd filled the cups. He sipped some of the tea, and then said, "The evidence bag contains something the police found in Clarence Harshaw's apartment. A cardboard box, and in it two wax figures in a distinctly embarrassing position, tied together with seven pieces of green thread and wrapped in a piece of green silk. Yes, it's a love spell of a classic type."

Ariel's brow wrinkled, and then she understood. "Oh."

"Exactly. It was no accident that Ms. Kozlowski and Mr. Benedetti fell head over heels in love the moment he came to her house to fix the plumbing. Once her brother and

Harshaw figured out where Captain Curdie's treasure was, what they needed most was some way to get Benedetti out of the way for a week or two, so they could break in, get the treasure, and cover their trail. Paul Chomski still isn't talking to the police, so we may never know which one of them thought of using a love spell to make that happen, but it's clear enough that Chomski deliberately loosened the drain pipe to let water get into the wall, and then suggested that his sister call Mr. Benedetti to fix it."

Ariel began to nod slowly. "I bet they were planning on getting the treasure while Teresa and Phil were away on their honeymoon."

"Very likely, yes. If Theophilus hadn't come back and forced Harshaw to try something desperate in a hurry, they might well have gotten away with it. As it is, the police gave the box and its contents to me and asked me to take care of it. Thus the perplexity."

Ariel sipped some of her tea. "What do you do with something like that?"

"It depends entirely on the circumstances. Normally it's a very bad idea to force two people into a relationship using magic, but once the spell is cast, that's a more complex matter. If either or both of the parties aren't satisfied with the effects, of course, it's good practice to break the spell and scatter the items, so that the two of them can go their separate ways. If there's a reasonable chance that they'll be happy together, though, it can be better to let things alone. In this case, that would probably amount to burying the box in the rose garden here. But I'm not entirely confident in my own judgment. I don't know the two of them as well as you do, and—" He shrugged. "My one brief venture into matrimony ended very badly, of course. So a second opinion is welcome."

Ariel considered that. After a minute or so, she said, "I think the box should go into the rose garden. The first few times I talked to Teresa she just felt tired and sad. Once she fell in love, it was like night and day. I don't think it would be fair to take that away from her. Besides, they've already sent out the wedding invitations." She motioned toward the mail.

Dr. Moravec extracted the card from the other letters and bills, opened and read it. "An October wedding," he said, with one raised eyebrow. "Still, I suppose there's no good reason for them to delay things. I'll put it on the calendar, and yes, we can bury the box in among the roses. I want to put in a new damask rose in the northeast corner anyway."

He put the card back atop the pile, drank more tea. "I should fill you in on another detail, too. The police found quite a collection of evidence in Paul Chomski's room, stolen items among them. He had the Ashmole shewstone, as I guessed."

"I thought Harshaw would have that."

Dr. Moravec shook his head. "He wouldn't have needed to buy a shewstone from Clarice Jackson's shop if that had been the case. For what it's worth, I suspect he and Chomski didn't trust each other any farther than they had to. That's probably why Harshaw kept the book but Chomski kept the shewstone: so one of them couldn't cheat the other out of half the treasure."

"I wonder if that's what Harshaw meant to do," Ariel said. "With the shewstone he bought from Aunt Clarice's store, I mean."

"Quite possibly yes." He finished his tea, poured himself another cup. "But I doubt anyone will ever know at this point."

He sat back, drank more tea. "The shewstone wasn't the only stolen item the police found in Chomski's room, though. There's been a string of daylight burglaries on the east side of Adocentyn over the last four years. They were odd crimes: just one or two expensive items taken, even when there was much more available. Never too close together, never with exactly the same modus operandi, and the goods that were stolen never showed up in pawnshops or any of the other places where professional burglars fence their take. Now the police know why. All of the stolen items were hidden away in Chomski's room.

As I thought, he didn't want the money. He wanted to have things just for himself, as he said."

"I saw something in the paper about felony charges," said Ariel.

"Seven counts of grand larceny," Dr. Moravec said. "At least as many counts of breaking and entering, and five or six more thefts of things that weren't expensive enough to cross the line into grand larceny. He'll be spending a very long time in prison."

"So was he the masked prowler, too?"

"The police can't confirm that but it's quite likely. Oh, and you were entirely correct about the library books. He had half a dozen items checked out from the fourth floor collection at the downtown branch. While Ms. Kozlowski was at work, her daughter was at school, and the son was with a neighbor because her brother was supposedly too sick to take care of him, Chomski was walking downtown to get books from the library, and diverting himself now and then with the occasional burglary. Also meeting with Harshaw and making plans."

"I wonder how they met."

"So do I. It might have been something as simple as looking for the same book on the fourth floor of the library."

Ariel refilled her teacup, settled back on the sofa. Her grandfather sipped from his own cup in silence. A brief moment of panic surged up as she considered what she was about to do, but she wrestled it into abeyance and said, "Can I ask a question?"

"Of course."

"It doesn't have anything to do with the case."

His gesture invited her to go on.

"I've finished *Dogme et Rituel de la Haute Magie*. Well, all but one and a half of the appendices. I don't understand a lot of it, but I think—" She had to push past another burst of panic. "I think I want to keep going. I think I want to learn magic—not just tobies and things, but the kind of magic you do—and I was wondering if you can teach me."

"Yes," he said: just the one syllable, nothing more. His eyes watched her, showed nothing of his thoughts.

She thought of Cassie's words then. "Do I have to ask you to do that?"

"Excellent. Yes, you do."

"Why?"

He leaned forward. "You should already know enough to answer that. Do you recall what Lévi wrote about will and imagination?" She nodded, and he went on. "The spell that changes a student into a mage is the most important and the most difficult magical working of all, but it follows the same laws as any other spell. First you must imagine yourself as a mage, and then you must will yourself to become one—and when you do that, not just once but day after day and year after year, the astral light flows into the form you've created and turns your imagination into a reality. So you have to ask. No one will ever offer you magical power, and if anyone claims that they can give it to you, you can assume that they're lying to you. You must ask for it, seek it, and achieve it yourself."

Ariel processed that. "Okay," she said, and gathered up her courage. "I want to become a mage and I want you to teach me how. Will you do that?"

"Yes. We can begin the training today."

She tried not to sag in sheer relief. "Thank you."

"You're most welcome." He settled back in his chair, and raised a hand. "Two points, though." One finger rose. "First, it's only fair for me to caution you that some of the training exercises will be duller than anything you've ever done before."

"Duller than listening to Mom tell me about everything I'm doing wrong with my life?"

"Yes. Also duller than the dullest class you ever sat through in high school."

Ariel gulped and then said, "Got it. Why?"

"Because you need to learn to perceive things that you've spent your entire life learning not to notice. You learn to do that the same way you learn to observe some very shy wild animal: by being very still and very silent, and waiting. It can take quite a while. That's a good half of what meditation is about, by the way."

"Okay, that makes sense."

"Keep that in mind a month from now, when the novelty's worn off and you'd rather have dental work without anesthetic than put in ten minutes of meditation every morning." Ariel choked with laughter, and he went on: "Trust me, you won't laugh then." He raised a second finger. "The other point is that there's a certain amount of latitude in the details of training. The same things have to be learned by each student, but there are various ways and means you can use to learn them. May I make a suggestion?"

"Sure."

"I gather from Saturday night's working that you have something of a talent for scrying in a crystal. That's not the most common skill, it has real advantages, and it so happens that you can do nearly all the basic training using a shewstone. There are other options, of course."

Ariel thought about that, and a slow smile spread over her face. "I think I'd like that. I think I'd like that a lot." Then: "Um, how big of a crystal do I need? I might have to save up for a while to afford anything more than a little one."

His gesture dismissed that concern. "Not to worry. There are traditional limits to what a teacher can or should do for a student, but I can certainly buy you a shewstone as a gift."

"Thank you. That's really nice of you."

He held up a hand, dismissing the words. "It's really nothing."

"Well, I'm still grateful. Deal."

He gave her a look with one raised eyebrow, then glanced up at the clock, which obligingly chimed to mark one of its odder cycles. "I trust Clarice has someone working the counter just now."

"Tasha Merriman," Ariel said. "She's on from two to six today."

"Highly convenient. Shall we? And then a late lunch at Lombroso's."

"Thank you. Seriously, thank you." She got to her feet, considered him. "You were waiting for me to ask, weren't you?"

"Of course." He unfolded himself from his armchair. "You mentioned a few months ago that you were interested in magic, but didn't know how much you wanted to learn. It's not wise to make assumptions in such cases, but I admit I had certain hopes."

"I'll do my best," she said as they started toward the door.